C0-ASB-934

"Sam Mclean, I could kiss you for what you did for my son tonight," Dani began.

Sam went absolutely still. The air between them whispered madly with electricity.

Dani flushed. "I mean, it was…I was…"

Sam's eyes glowed. "I like the way you put it the first time."

Moving slowly, he came to her side. His powerful shoulders gave the impression of strength and command, but the hand that reached out to touch her cheek was infinitely gentle.

As she stood in the living room, with the house redolent of the aroma of dinner and echoing with the sound of a child's bedtime prayers, Dani looked into this mystery man's eyes—the same man who poured ketchup on her roast beef hash and dried her dishes and made her heart race every time she looked at him—and realized something.

This must be what it's like to be married.

Dear Reader,

The holiday season is a time for family, love...and miracles! We have all this—and more!—for you this month in Silhouette Romance. So in the gift-giving spirit, we offer *you* these wonderful books by some of the genre's finest:

A workaholic executive finds a baby in his in-box and enlists the help of the sexy single mom next door in this month's BUNDLES OF JOY, *The Baby Came C.O.D.*, by RITA Award-winner Marie Ferrarella. *Both* hero and heroine are twins, and Marie tells their identical siblings' stories in *Desperately Seeking Twin*, out this month in our Yours Truly line.

Favorite author Elizabeth August continues our MEN! promotion with *Paternal Instincts*. This latest installment in her SMYTHESHIRE, MASSACHUSETTS series features an irresistible lone wolf turned doting dad! As a special treat, Carolyn Zane's sizzling family drama, THE BRUBAKER BRIDES, continues with *His Brother's Intended Bride*—the title says it all!

Completing the month are *three* classic holiday romances. A world-weary hunk becomes *The Dad Who Saved Christmas* in this magical tale by Karen Rose Smith. Discover *The Drifter's Gift* in RITA Award-winning author Lauryn Chandler's emotional story. Finally, debut author Zena Valentine weaves a tale of transformation—and miracles—in *From Humbug to Holiday Bride*.

So treat yourself this month—and every month!—to Silhouette Romance!

Happy holidays,

Joan Marlow Golan
Senior Editor

Please address questions and book requests to:
Silhouette Reader Service
U.S.: 3010 Walden Ave., P.O. Box 1325, Buffalo, NY 14269
Canadian: P.O. Box 609, Fort Erie, Ont. L2A 5X3

THE DRIFTER'S
$\mathcal{G}$IFT

Lauryn Chandler

Silhouette
R O M A N C E™
Published by Silhouette Books
America's Publisher of Contemporary Romance

If you purchased this book without a cover you should be aware
that this book is stolen property. It was reported as "unsold and
destroyed" to the publisher, and neither the author nor the
publisher has received any payment for this "stripped book."

With deep gratitude to Lynda Curnyn, editor, for her kindness and
care in helping me finish this book.
Dedicated to Tim Blough—old friend, new husband!—whose arms
are the warmest place I know.
And to Laura Lea Seidenberg Warren, 1930-1997. You gave me
life and, with the courage of a lion, the gentleness of a lamb,
showed me how to live it. How I miss you. *L'chaim*, Little Lady.
To life.

 SILHOUETTE BOOKS

ISBN 0-373-19268-1

THE DRIFTER'S GIFT

Copyright © 1997 by Wendy Warren

All rights reserved. Except for use in any review, the reproduction
or utilization of this work in whole or in part in any form by any
electronic, mechanical or other means, now known or hereafter
invented, including xerography, photocopying and recording, or in
any information storage or retrieval system, is forbidden without
the written permission of the editorial office, Silhouette Books,
300 East 42nd Street, New York, NY 10017 U.S.A.

All characters in this book have no existence outside the imagination of
the author and have no relation whatsoever to anyone bearing the same
name or names. They are not even distantly inspired by any individual
known or unknown to the author, and all incidents are pure invention.

This edition published by arrangement with Harlequin Books S.A.

® and TM are trademarks of Harlequin Books S.A., used under license.
Trademarks indicated with ® are registered in the United States Patent
and Trademark Office, the Canadian Trade Marks Office and in other
countries.

Printed in U.S.A.

Books by Lauryn Chandler

Silhouette Romance

Mr. Wright #936
Romantics Anonymous #981
Oh, Baby! #1033
Her Very Own Husband #1148
Just Say I Do #1236
The Drifter's Gift #1268

LAURYN CHANDLER

Originally from California, Lauryn now lives in the beautiful Pacific Northwest, where she can look out her window and see deer walking down the street. She holds a B.A. in Drama, and when not writing, she enjoys spending time with her family and husband, going for long hikes with her dogs and finding new ways to cheat at Crazy Eights.

Lauryn is the recipient of the 1995 Romance Writers of America RITA Award for Best Traditional Romance.

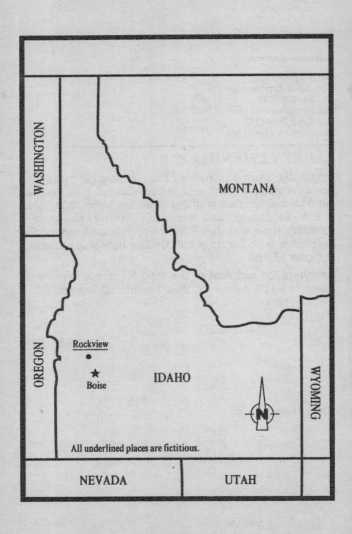

WASHINGTON

MONTANA

OREGON

Rockview
●

★
Boise

IDAHO

WYOMING

All underlined places are fictitious.

NEVADA

UTAH

Prologue

San Bernardino, California

"Look, Daddy, Teacher says every time a bell rings another angel gets his wings."

"That's right. That's right! Atta boy, Clarence."

The last lines of *It's a Wonderful Life* competed with the phlegmy hiss of a decrepit heating unit in the corner of Sam Mclean's motel room.

Sam gazed inexpressively at the black and white TV as Jimmy Stewart, Donna Reed and a gaggle of Hollywood extras gathered around a Christmas tree for a rousing chorus of "Auld Lang Syne."

Shifting on the lumpy, coarse motel mattress, Sam grunted. TV programmers were a sadistic bunch. Barely through one holiday, and they couldn't wait to remind you there was another panting in the wings.

Reaching for the small plastic bottle on his nightstand, he glanced at the digital clock—the most modern gadget in the room—and sighed. Four hours to go until midnight. Officially, it was still Thanksgiving.

Holding the vial of pills in his right hand, he used his thumb to pop off the plastic top. He was getting good at this—could hold, open, hang on to the top and even close the bottle again with just one hand. It was a little game he played with himself, a talent he'd perfected with lots of practice and which left his other hand conveniently free for the water chaser.

Shaking two oblong white pills into his mouth, he reached for the glass of tap water he kept by the bed, swallowed and set everything on the nightstand. Leaning on his left hip, he winced. And swore. Once again he'd waited too long to take the painkillers.

The fact that the meds were supposed to be ingested with food could not persuade him to return to the dinner he'd abandoned two hours earlier. Pressed turkey, gravy that was the same bright yellow as the bugs smashed on his windshield, and cubes of damp bread that tasted like they'd been stuck together with Elmer's White Glue—the turkey special from Hungry Harry's Country Diner made mess hall slop look like five-star cuisine.

Gripping the handle of the handsome walnut cane his outfit had given him the day he was discharged from the base hospital, Sam sat up and carefully lowered his feet to the floor.

Jeez!

Every move made him feel like he was being stabbed from the inside out.

He stood, gained his bearings and walked—or

rather limped—to the window, passing the small round table that held his aborted meal as he went. Lying open next to a cup of piss-poor black coffee was the letter his friend Joseph Lawson had sent one week before Sam's discharge.

Come to Idaho, Joe had written. *Hang out for awhile. Take some time before you make any major decisions. And remember, there's a job waiting at Lawson's.* Lawson's, the family store Joe had taken over when his father passed away. *Mom and the girls would love to see you again. Hell, why spend the holidays alone?*

Sam adjusted his body, leaning his shoulder against the wall so his better, right leg would bear most of his weight. He ignored the remaining pain as best he could while he stared at the hazy moon.

Starless. There were too many streetlights, too much residual pollution to see the heavens here, even at night. He reached up to rub his eyes, then passed his hand over his cheeks and chin. Both were stubble free. Out of sheer habit he'd shaved this afternoon.

As a sergeant first class in the United States Armed Forces, he had spent his holidays on base or, when he hadn't been able to avoid it, at the home of another officer. On those occasions, he'd been surrounded by laughter, good food, bright conversation.

He hadn't felt any less alone then than he did right now.

Across the street, a red neon light blinked Bar. Sam felt his leg throb in cadence with the pulsing light, the pain an ever-present reminder that his days as a platoon leader were over. For thirteen years of service, he had belonged. If not to someone, then at least to someplace, something.

Now what? A desk job, pushing paper all day?

"Damn." Sam whacked his cane against the wall with enough force to chip the plaster. An overwhelming sense of fruitlessness, an awful, gnawing emptiness assailed him. Without his work, who was he?

Once more his gaze fell to the letter he'd been carrying around for three weeks. *There's a job waiting at Lawson's.*

He rubbed his temples. Maybe. At least it would be somewhere to go. A way to pass the time while he figured out what to do with the rest of his life.

For a moment, he closed his eyes. The pain that washed through him this time had little to do with his leg.

When the wall heater gave a particularly nasty belch, Sam lifted his head and stared out the window, disappointed by the filmy clouds that veiled the face of the moon. Tired, he laid his forehead against the wall and came to a decision, if only to end his infernal waffling.

Maybe there would be stars in Idaho.

Chapter One

Rockview, Idaho
Thanksgiving

"**P**lay the petunia game!"

Wriggling into the bottoms of his favorite superhero pajamas, Timmy Harmon fell back on his soft bed and thrust his bare feet in the air.

"Pick a petunia, Mommy."

Grinning, Dani tugged her son until he was lying with his rump snuggled against her thigh, his rosy toes close enough for her to kiss. Timmy folded his hands on his belly and giggled. The petunia game was one of his favorites. It made the ritual of a nighttime bath almost worthwhile.

Bending toward her smiling five-year-old, Dani wiggled each little toe in turn. "One petunia for Timmy's mother to pick. Two petunias for Mommy to pick..." She remembered her mother playing the silly, simple game with her. She'd loved it then as much as Timmy did now.

When she'd wriggled the last toe, Dani bent to place a noisy kiss on the arch of each child-size foot. Curled lovingly around his ankle, her fingers lingered a bit longer than usual tonight.

From the first booties she'd put on him to the new blue and red sneakers he'd chosen himself for kindergarten, Dani always felt a bittersweet stir of anticipation when she looked at her little boy's feet, so small, so wonderfully, restlessly eager. And growing so quickly.

Patting the soft skin of his instep, Dani released her hold and reached for a pair of socks still warm from the dryer. She held them up. "It's cold tonight. You want socks?"

Timmy nodded. In the glow from the teddy bear lamp on the nightstand, her son's hair was as russet as her own.

Dani rolled the blue cotton socks over his feet, tickling the arches as she went, filling with pleasure when he dissolved into giggles.

When the socks were in place, Timmy sat up on his knees. "Okay, Mommy, you go out now."

"You haven't said your prayers yet."

"I know, but I'm going to do it myself tonight."

I can do it was becoming an increasingly common refrain around their house, but rarely at bedtime. Resisting the urge to show her disappointment, Dani smiled and stood.

"Okay, pup." She bent, kissing his downy cheek. "Lights out when you're through."

A stack of clean, folded towels awaited her atop

the dryer, and more laundry tumbled inside, so Dani decided to busy herself with hausfrau duties until her own bedtime.

On her way to the hall closet, she glanced into the living room and saw her pop sitting on the couch, just as she and Timmy had left him, head back against the cushion, neck arched, mouth open wide as he snored. His hands lay on his lap, palms up— an unconscious yogi.

From the TV came the sound of voices raised in song. "Auld Lang Syne." Dani grinned. The last scene in *It's a Wonderful Life*. He'd watched that weepy old flick twice already this holiday season, and if she knew her father, he'd watch it twice more before Christmas. He saw things so simply, her sweet dad. Jimmy Stewart was still the best actor going, Donna Reed was the cutest girl, pumpkin pie with whipped cream turned a meal into a feast and…it was a wonderful life.

Pressing her face against the top towel of the stack she carried, Dani let the material absorb her deep sigh. She stood a moment longer, watching her father's glasses slip by tiny degrees as he snored, then she moved down the hall.

When she reached Timmy's door, she stopped. Prayers usually lasted all of thirty seconds—forty if there was a pet frog involved—so the muffled sounds coming from her son's room drew her like a magnet. Sidling alongside the door, she peeked in. The teddy bear lamp was turned off. A night-light provided the only illumination. Timmy spoke to a group of toy figures he'd assembled.

"One more glass of water, that's all." He lowered

his voice to as deep a register as he could manage—a child's version of a baritone.

"You were a good boy today." He jiggled one of the toys, making it speak. "Tomorrow you can have a treat. We'll go see Santa Claus. Would you like that?" he asked a figure lying on his pillow and in his own voice responded, "Oh, boy! And Mommy will make cookies. Them ones Santa likes."

"Yes, pup," he answered in the deep, manly voice again. "Now go to sleep. Mommy and I will watch you."

Mommy and I? Dani leaned farther around the door. Timmy returned to his normal register. "Kiss Mommy," he commanded the toy in his right hand—the father. Bringing the two figures together until they clacked heads, he made a noisy sucking sound. "Now tell Mommy you love her." And once more in the baritone, "I love you. Now go to sleep."

Walking his makeshift family across the bed, he seated them on the nightstand, positioning the plastic figures so that the two parents were standing protectively over their son.

Tucking himself beneath the quilt, Timmy curled up on his side, eyes open, curly head craned, watching his "family" watch him.

Frozen in the doorway, Dani forgot she was holding towels until the stack began to topple. Making a quick, noiseless save, she backed into the hall. Her steps to the closet were so automatic she barely registered she was taking them.

In the living room, her father's snoring intensified to buzz-saw decibels. Dani stowed the towels, her hands shaking, her movements clumsy. Jelly seemed to have replaced the bones in her knees.

She remembered the promise she'd made her son the day they'd left the hospital together—she lonely and scared at twenty-three, he a tiny, defenseless bundle wrapped in her arms. *We'll be a family, you and I. I promise.*

Pressing her palms against the oft-painted panel of the closet door, Dani touched her forehead to the wood and squeezed her eyes tight. Oh, God, had she failed? They were a family, weren't they? She hadn't blown it too badly yet, had she?

She certainly hadn't meant to wind up broke in the boondocks of Idaho, in a house that was a paint job away from dilapidated, on a farm that barely supported itself. She hadn't meant for them to be alone on Thanksgiving or Christmas or New Year's.

Hearing the sudden snort that signaled her father wakening from his nap, Dani pushed away from the closet, wiped her eyes and hurried into her bedroom. She closed the door softly behind her, moving toward the window without flipping on the light.

With the curtains drawn, moonlight cast silver beams into the room. Dani stood close to the cold glass, arms wrapped around her waist, staring out.

I should have moved to Los Angeles, some city where the local chapter of Parents Without Partners is bigger than the PTA.

This time her sigh was ragged and tired. It fogged the glass. Everywhere she looked, stars seemed to be winking.

"Whatever the joke is, I wish you'd let me in on it," she whispered to the cosmos.

Somewhere under this very same sky were people who still made wishes, people who still believed. She'd been like that once, dreaming with her eyes wide open. That's what she wanted for her son—enough innocence to believe that dreams came true. Five was too young yet to learn about life's disappointments.

Shivering inside her thick sweater, Dani hugged herself more tightly. What, she wondered, could this nighttime sky with its moon and its stars and its mystery have to offer a not-so-young-anymore single mother who'd stopped believing in wishes long ago?

Letting her hands drift up until they were linked beneath her chin, she closed her eyes. And then, because she had no idea what else to do, for the first time in more years than Dani could remember, she prayed.

"Girl, you are out of your gourd!"

"Shh, Pop, Timmy'll hear you." From the kitchen doorway, Dani glanced into the living room to check on her son, who was still engrossed in running his dump truck up and down the legs of their sofa. His pliant lips sputtered as he made engine sounds.

Turning toward the oven, Dani removed a pan of oatmeal-coconut crunch cookies.

"Want coffee?" she asked her father. "There's one cup left in the pot."

Eugene Harmon shook his head. "Nope. I had three cups already. Too much caffeine." He watched Dani cross to the fridge to pour herself a glass of orange juice. "'Course, I don't want it to go to waste if you're not going to have any." He rose with his mug. "Pour it in there."

Blinking rapidly behind his glasses, Gene hitched his trousers higher on his waist—his characteristic gesture when he anticipated something enjoyable. Dani smiled. Timmy had adopted the same habit of late.

"Want one of these?" Reaching for the giant cookies, she pulled her hand back abruptly and affected an innocent look. "Oh, sorry, Pop. I forgot, you're cutting back on sugar, too, aren't you?"

Gene pulled a dish from one of the cabinets. Brown eyes shining as he acknowledged the gibe, he tapped the center of the chipped china dessert plate. "Just put it right there."

They settled at the breakfast table, and Dani began to fidget, plucking at a piece of orange pulp that was stuck to the rim of her glass.

"You know, it's not such a bad idea when you think about it," she said hesitantly, easing back to the topic at hand. She raised her eyes to her father's. Behind wire-framed glasses, Gene regarded his daughter stonily, and Dani squirmed with the need to defend the decision she'd come to during the night. "Pop, how many great marriages do you know of? I mean really great ones. Love affairs. Name three off the top of your head."

Gene popped a piece of cookie into his mouth, taking an excessively long time to chew. "Antony and Cleopatra."

"*Live* people."

Reaching for his coffee, he frowned.

"See?" Dani countered. "Bet you can't name

even one." Digging peanut butter from a groove in the pine table, she smiled sadly. "Me, either. Except for you and Mom."

Rubbing his nose where long ago his glasses had left a permanent indentation, Gene nodded. He spoke infrequently of his late wife, but Dani knew he thought of her often.

"You and Mom used to laugh so much. I remember thinking you were telling her jokes."

Gene smiled. "Sometimes I was." They sat quietly a moment, then he offered, "You could have that, too. You're so pretty, honey. And smart. Maybe I never told you that enough."

"Yes, you did." Dani hated the look of uncertainty on her father's face. "You did everything just right, Pop."

"Then don't rush into anything," he cautioned, referring to the plan she'd related to him this morning. "Marriage is hard work. Without love—"

"I'd rather have commitment without love than love without commitment. And don't tell me I can have both." Already primed to utter exactly those words, Eugene's mouth snapped shut. "I'm twenty-eight years old, and I have a child. I don't have the time to chase rainbows. I don't have the energy."

"You could still meet someone...the natural way."

Wincing at the clear implication that what she was about to do was highly *un*natural, Dani countered, "Where am I going to meet someone in Rockview?"

Fewer than a thousand people lived in the historic mining town, most of them married. Or incontinent. "Face it, Pop, when we went eeny-meeny-miney-mo with that map, we landed in a town that makes Noah's Ark look like a singles' cruise.''

"You could get out more. Take a girlfriend and drive into Boise. Maybe there's someplace there you could go dancing.'' His inflection rose with hopefulness.

Dancing. After nine or ten hours of work every day, Dani's feet hurt just thinking about it. "I don't want to pick someone up at a dance. Or have them try to pick me up. I like my idea better.''

She splayed her hands across the scarred top of the pine table. There was a business-size white envelope next to the ceramic salt shaker. Gene's gaze followed hers, and his expression grew more troubled. With an effort, Dani steeled herself to proceed even in the face of her father's uneasiness. Even in the face of her own.

Inside that envelope was her chance to create a family for her son. Mentally, she reviewed the words she'd written and had read to her father early this morning.

A home for the holidays

Small family on small farm seeks man willing to make our house his home. Must love kids and hard work. Clean living, solid background with work and personal references required. Ninety-day trial period leading to legal union. Serious inquiries only.

"I got most of my cars through the newspaper,'' Gene grumbled. "Half of 'em were lemons.''

Dani mustered a smile. "That's why I'm insisting on a trial period. It's like a three-month test drive."

Gene found little humor in the situation. He shook his head, then stood. "Well. We better get going if we're going to make it to Lawson's in time to see Santa."

The abrupt change in topic threw Dani off stride. She'd intended to talk until Pop saw things her way. But he'd always been the kind of father who let his daughter make her own mistakes. And she'd made some dillies. Praying this wasn't going to be another of them, Dani picked up the envelope and tucked it in the pocket of her cardigan. Later, she would ask Pop to run the ad over to the *Tribune* office while she did the grocery shopping. That way she'd have no chance to get cold feet. The *County Trib* was circulated all over the state. Her ad would get a lot of play.

"I'll get Timmy. Thanks for coming with us, Pop. These outings with you mean the world to him."

Gene waved her gratitude away. "He's my grandson, isn't he? Better make him put on his mittens. Looks like it may snow again."

Dani rose. Instead of proceeding to the living room, she laid a hand on Gene's arm. "It won't be just anybody. If the right person doesn't come along, then we'll just keep doing what we're doing. But I have to try, Dad. For Timmy."

Gene covered her hand with his and nodded.

Turning, Dani called out to her son. "Grab your coat and your mittens, pup. We're going to visit Santa!"

Chapter Two

In all his thirty-two years, Sam had never seen so many runny noses.

Seated on an oversize armchair of cheap black vinyl and wood that was spray-painted gold, he gazed at the ocean of children before him and felt like he'd been sacrificed to an alien nation.

They were lined up in an endless stream, dozens of them, not a one taller than its mother's hip and as far as Sam could tell, each doing the same thing— wiping its nose on its sleeve and waiting to sit on *his* lap.

The minute—the very instant—he saw his old friend Joe Lawson, he would tell the back-stabbing lummox exactly what he could do with this "job." *Come to Idaho, buddy.... Always a place for you at Lawson's, pal....* Sam's gloved hand clenched. Wiseacre, joking son of a—

"We're ready, Santa!" A woman dressed in a

short green tunic, green tights and ankle boots gave him an enthusiastic thumbs-up. Sam winced on her behalf. She looked like a cross between an elf and the label on a can of peas. Behind the stiff, scratchy beard the Lawson's Superstore management had handed him, Sam gave a brief, sorry shake of his head. He doubted he looked any more dignified than she.

"Testing…" The woman tapped a microphone. She whispered, but her voice carried. "One, two, three, testing…" Satisfied the PA system was up and running, she motioned for quiet—got none—and proceeded.

"Greetings, shoppers!" she boomed into the mike. "Welcome to Lawson's Superstore's third annual holiday extravaganza!" Scattered applause. "A month-long schedule of sensational seasonal events designed to make your holiday shopping spectacular!"

Unbelievable. Sam scanned the crowd while Ms. Elf held for cheers. A few people clapped. A baby cried. Undaunted, she continued. "Only three weeks to Christmas, shoppers, and you know what that means. All throughout the store today and every day between now and December twenty-fifth, you'll find *super*-phenomenal savings on a wide variety of products, everything from bulk carrots in our produce section—" she pointed east "—to holiday tablecloths and place mats in housewares, aisle four. And while you're shopping, shoppers, don't forget that we have a special treat for little customers." She grinned. "That's right, he's here—"

Oh, brother. Beneath the mountain of foam padding that covered his stomach, Sam felt his gut clench. *I swear to God, the next time someone offers me work—*

"—in Lawson's Holiday Village—" the elf warmed her audience like a veteran Ed McMahon, and this time the children screamed with pleasure "—straight from the North Pole—"

Joe, you son of a bitch.

"Moms and dads, boys and girls—" she flung out an arm "—the one, the only...*Santa Claus!*"

Trapped, gulled, conned into playing a part as foreign to him as Bermuda shorts to a polar bear, Sam raised a white-gloved hand. His smile felt as frozen as his vocal cords, his lips barely moved, as he attempted that immortal refrain.

"Ho. Ho. Ho."

Three hours later, the line of children had dwindled considerably, but both of Sam's legs were killing him. He'd been seating the kids on his uninjured right thigh, which was now almost as sore as his left.

At present, a little girl named Sarah Jean was running through a list of requests that would bankrupt her parents within an hour.

"...and a Malibu Barbie, Hunchback of Notre Dame lunch box—I *don't* like Pocahontas anymore..."

Sam nodded. Discreetly, he thought, he lifted his gaze to where the elf stood, checking the flash on the camera she used to capture these special holiday moments—for three bucks a pop. It was her job to signal when a kid's five minutes with Santa were up. Sarah Jean, he was sure, had to be pressing the limit.

"Are you listening?" The pigtailed girl caught him shifting his focus.

Sam returned the malevolent stare. "Yeah. You don't like Pocahontas."

Looking at him suspiciously, Sarah Jean resumed her request concert. With each new mention of a toy, she swung her patent-leather shoes into Sam's shin. He'd asked her twice already not to do that.

"Sarah Jean," he said once again, "I told you, don't kick Santa."

The little girl glared at him. "I don't like you. The other Santas are better. I went to Boise and that Santa told me I'd get everything I deserved for Christmas."

For the first time that day, Sam allowed a genuine smile beneath the bushy mustache. "I'm sure he's right." At last his co-worker gave him the high sign. Thank God. "Okay, kid. Turn around and face the elf."

A bright flash caught them both, then Sarah Jean hopped off his knee and scurried toward her mother, casting suspicious glances at Sam.

Mildly repentant, he sighed. He was probably ruining Joe's business, giving dozens of innocent Idaho youths a fear of Santa Claus—and their parents a fear of shopping at Lawson's.

Ten children remained in line. Rubbing his leg, Sam resolved to be as Santalike as possible for the next fifty minutes. The next child up, a little boy, approached and stood at his knee.

For several moments—long ones, Sam thought— he and the kid just stared at each other.

Thick, wavy red hair hugged the boy's head like a woolly cap. Freckles splattered the bridge of his nose. Dressed warmly in crisp, neatly pressed clothes and brightly colored tennis shoes, he was just the kind of kid Sam remembered his friends picking on in grade school. The kind of kid who *looked* well-mothered.

Thrusting out a flannel-covered arm, the little guy held up a paper lunch bag. "These are for you. My mommy made 'em. She says they're the kind you like."

Accepting the bag, Sam opened it to examine the contents. The aroma of butter and brown sugar drifted up. Four very large, very thick golden brown cookies that begged tasting rested inside.

"The kind *I* like?" he murmured. He didn't doubt it for a minute. Breaking his own rule—the less contact with parents, the better—he glanced up, searching almost unwillingly for this boy's mother. She was easy to find.

"I asked her to put in extra for the reindeers, but she says no dessert for them because they can't brush their teeth. Do reindeers have very big teeth?"

Sam nodded.

Her hair was like fire, as red as her son's. It waved thickly back from her forehead, exposing a gentle widow's peak and skin as creamy and subtly toned as her hair was bright. She stood next to an older man, too old, Sam thought, to be the boy's father. Her gaze was all for her son.

She would stand out in any crowd. Tall and slender, with refined features he could easily imagine on the cover of a magazine, she looked like a woman who belonged in a city—at the theater, in an elegant restaurant, dressed to the nines.

Then she smiled at her child, and Sam had no trouble picturing her in jeans in her kitchen, making snacks for Santa.

All of a sudden, he had the overwhelming urge to taste one of the cookies, just so he could tell her how good they were.

A light tug strained his sleeve. "Should I get on your lap now?"

"Yeah." Rolling up the bag, Sam looked for somewhere to stow it, settling for behind his chair, next to the cane he was still using. "Thanks," he said. "Tell your mom...thanks."

"Okay." The youngster nodded, then climbed onto Sam's lap.

"What's your name?"

"Timmy Harmon."

"How old are you, Tim?"

"Five."

"Five." Sam nodded. "Pretty big for five, aren't you?"

It wasn't true, not by a long shot, but it puffed Timmy Harmon up like a helium balloon in a Thanksgiving parade.

"I guess," he answered proudly, his teeth showing in a white line interrupted by a couple of empty spaces, like missing slats in a picket fence.

Sam smiled a little. This kid was easy to please. Remembering his Santa dialogue, he asked, "Have you been a good boy this year?"

Timmy considered the question. "Uh-huh. I think. 'Cept I forgot to pick up my building blocks."

The other half of Sam's mouth joined his smile. "That doesn't sound too bad. So, what do you want

Santa to bring you for Christmas?'' The words rolled more easily than they had all day.

Most of the other children had answered that question immediately, but Timmy merely sat on Sam's knee, studying him. ''Does your beard hurt?'' Timmy reached up to pat the white whiskers and frowned. ''Feels like the sweater Mrs. Richter gave me.''

''Mrs. Richter?''

''She lives on our block. I have to say thank-you even if I'm never gonna wear it.'' Gently, he poked at the space between Sam's lower lip and the top of the beard. ''How come your beard's not stuck to your face?''

From the corner of his eye, Sam saw the elf give him the speed-it-up signal.

''Listen, Tim. I want to make sure you get what you want for Christmas, so why don't you tell me what's on your list?''

The boy continued to look at him quizzically. ''Are you the for-real Santa?'' He sounded doubtful.

Not sure whether to be insulted or relieved, Sam allowed himself a second to think. Getting two dozen troops to march in a straight line was nothing compared to this Santa stuff.

What if he admitted he was just a guy in a cheap velvet suit? Would he ruin the kid's psyche forever?

Another glance into the candid auburn-lashed eyes, and the answer seemed to come out unbidden. ''No, I'm not the real Santa.'' Disappointment flashed across Tim's face. ''But I know him.'' *Oh, jeez! Did I really say that?*

''Are you guys friends?''

"Yeah. We're friends. We…raced reindeer to-gether…in Alaska." *Oh, boy.*

Timmy seemed more interested in Sam's having lived in Alaska than he was in the concept of reindeer racing. Sam answered eager questions about Eskimos and igloos, then saw the elf give him an emphatic wind-it-up. He ignored her.

"Where's the for-real Santa right now?"

"Right now?" Sam frowned. "He's at the North Pole. Resting. He's got to be up all night, you know, on Christmas Eve, and…well, he's not getting any younger."

"Like my granpop." Timmy nodded. "He goes to bed at night sometimes even before I do. How old is Santa Claus?"

"Older than anyone I've ever met," Sam acknowledged. "If you tell me what you want for Christmas, I'll make sure he hears all about it."

Timmy got quiet then, plucking at the broad brass clasp of Sam's belt, looking up with wide, achingly innocent eyes.

Before the little boy could respond, the lady elf approached with a strained smile. Placing both hands on her jutting green-stockinged knees, she leaned forward and spoke to Timmy. "You're getting along so well with Santa, aren't you? And I hate to interrupt, but there are lots of other little boys and girls who want to speak with him, too. We can't take all his time." Her syrupy voice merely underscored her irritation.

Immediately, Timmy looked like he was afraid he'd done something wrong. Sam felt a surge of very un-Santalike anger.

"Give us a moment, would you, please?" he requested, more politely, he thought, than she deserved.

"Oh, now—" she wagged a finger at Sam "—it isn't fair to the other children in line to make them wait."

"We'll be done in a minute."

Smiling wider, the elf moved to stand directly in front of them so the parents could not see their exchange. "My lunch hour was thirty minutes ago. I have signaled you three times. I know you saw me—"

"Hey! Elf Lady," Sam interrupted. "We're not done yet. When we are, *I'll* signal *you.*"

Timmy watched with openmouthed awe as the woman blinked several times, recovered enough to glare at Sam, then turned and stalked to her station.

"She's mad," the little boy breathed.

"Forget about her," Sam instructed. "She's not a real elf. So what is it you want this year?"

Timmy's little legs began to swing nervously. Sam winced when the boy connected with his shin. Gently, he placed a hand on Timmy's knees. "What do you say, champ? What do you want? Some of the kids have been asking for Power Rangers. They were about your age, I think. You want one of those?"

Timmy shook his head.

"No, huh? Got something else in mind?"

Hesitantly, the boy nodded.

"Okay. Let 'er rip."

Gaze lowered, Timmy Harmon mumbled something Sam couldn't understand. "Say it again?"

Timmy raised his eyes. "I want a daddy."

Hell.

Oh, how Sam wished he'd listened to the damn elf. Feeling his throat freeze, he wondered what he could say. *I'm sure your mommy will get you one?*

Involuntarily, his eyes fastened on the boy's mother. The soft smile was still in place. She was standing near the exit, too far away to hear what was being said, particularly with the piped-in holiday Muzak, but she looked curious, apparently aware that he was taking more time with her son than he had with the others.

"Where's your daddy?"

Timmy folded his hands neatly in his lap. His cheeks were pink. The small shoulders lifted in a shrug.

Well, you had no business asking that, Mclean, none at all. But he wondered. He definitely wondered.

A woman who made cookies for her son to give to Santa, who had hair like autumn, skin like winter and—if they were anything like her son's—eyes green as summer leaves...had someone walked away from that? And from this boy?

Keep your mind on the job.

"Listen," he began. He no intention of implying that Santa could dish up dads for Christmas. "Fathers...you know, they aren't all they're cracked up to be. I mean, without one you only get yelled at half as much, right?" The smile he attempted fell flat.

His logic made no impression on Timmy, who shrugged again, then asked, "Will you tell Santa?"

Sam looked at the little fellow, so hopeful, so tentative. To say he was out of his element didn't begin to describe the ineptitude Sam felt. What could he say? "I'll tell him."

Timmy stared at Sam a long time. *Probably wondering if he should trust a guy who admits to wearing a fake beard.*

Sliding off Sam's lap to stand at his knee, the child issued a very polite thank-you, then turned and ran off.

The exit from Santa's Holiday Village was a green runner between two rows of painted cardboard pine trees. Timmy got about halfway down the twenty-five-foot walkway before another child approached for an audience. Sam smiled absently at the little girl, lifting her to his knee. He kept his eyes on Timmy.

At the end of the makeshift aisle, Timmy jogged right, running headlong for his mother and the man Sam guessed was Granpop. The woman received her son by holding out her arm, pulling him in for a quick hug and bending low to speak to him. When she straightened again, she looked directly at Sam and smiled.

It was a thank-you, nothing more, nothing less.

It turned her face into a work of art.

Sam continued to stare after she and her family had walked away. He spent the next forty minutes uttering Santa-isms and a half hour after that had changed out of his costume. He exited the employee lounge, then halted as abruptly as his bum leg would allow.

Facing him on the opposite side of the wide hall was a community bulletin board crowded with notices about lost dogs, skis for sale and jobs wanted.

Standing in front of the board were Timmy Harmon and his grandfather.

"Put on a blue one," Timmy instructed, bouncing with approval when his grandfather stabbed a colored thumbtack into the corkboard.

"All right, that'll do it." Nodding, the older man stood to study the three-by-five card he'd posted. "She's going to thank me for this. Eventually."

He put a hand on top of Timmy's red head. "Let's see if your mother's through shopping yet. She's happier in a market than a gopher in a hole."

Timmy giggled, and they moved off. Sam wondered if the little boy would recognize him as they passed, but he was chattering up a storm and didn't even glance Sam's way. Apparently, out of the red suit Sam was just a stranger with a cane—and Timmy's mother's cookies in a brown paper bag tucked in his hand.

Thinking of the cookies drew a growl from his stomach.

Thinking of Timmy's mother drew him to the bulletin board.

He felt like a voyeur, looking at a board in which he took no interest except for the small card with the blue thumbtack at the top. His eyes first widened, then narrowed as he read the message.

WANTED

Man to work on small organic farm. Able to relocate and live on premises for room, board (good food!) and small stipend with potential for future partnership. Must like children. Please reply to Gene, 555-1807

Sam leaned on his cane, staring at the notice. Seemed Timmy wasn't the only one who thought they needed a man around the house.

Gazing down the hall, he felt a stirring of interest he hadn't felt for anything in a long while.

When his stomach spoke up again, he unrolled the bag of cookies, reached in and extracted one thick, uniformly browned circle. He planned to have a late lunch or early dinner in the coffee shop next to his motel room, but in the meantime—

The first bite nearly brought a tear to his eye. He tasted oats and brown sugar. He tasted coconut and pecans and…home.

Standing in front of the bulletin board, he chewed slowly, letting the taste—and the feeling—linger.

Home. It had been a long time. It seemed like forever.

Sam stayed where he was until a couple of employees emerged from the lounge, arguing about which of the town's two movie theaters they should visit. Coming back to his surroundings, he pretended to scan the board. But his gaze never strayed, really, his attention never shifted, from the card stuck to the board with a blue thumbtack.

Chapter Three

Leaning back in a desk chair barely large enough to support his big frame, Joe Lawson pointed a finger at his old buddy Sam and nodded. "You look good in a full beard. The white tended to age you, but..." He shrugged and a slow, deliberate grin spread across his amiable features.

Closing the door behind him, Sam entered his friend's office with an expression more befitting the Grim Reaper than Santa Claus.

"Now, Sammy—" Joe held up a hand as Sam limped into the room "—if I didn't know better, I'd say you were peeved. And that can't be, because Old St. Nick is a jolly old soul." Clasping his hands behind his head, Joe kicked his feet up on the desk and frowned. "Or is that Frosty the Snowman?"

One hundred percent certain now that the Santa job had been Joe Lawson's pathetic attempt at a practical joke, Sam shook his head.

"Neither," he corrected, approaching the desk. "Old King Cole was a *merry* old soul." Smiling, he cocked his head. "I don't suppose you remember the one about Humpty Dumpty?"

"Humpty Dumpty?" Joe looked bemused.

"Yeah. How did that go?"

"You're kidding."

"No." Resting his cane against the desk, Sam folded his arms. "Recite it."

Shrugging at his friend's sudden interest in nursery rhymes, Joe recited, "Humpty Dumpty sat on a wall, Humpty Dumpty had a great— Hey!"

Humpty Dumpty had a great fall, but not as great as the spill Joe took when Sam lifted his feet off the desk and shoved him backward. The cushy leather chair in which Joe liked to rock back listed all the way, right down to the floor, with Joe in it.

The big man's hard belly bounced. Laughter rolled from his barrel chest.

Sam took a seat in a chair on the opposite side of the desk and let a genuine—albeit reluctant—smile curve his lips. "I should have known better than to put that suit on this morning. When they said you wanted me to play Santa, I thought it was a real job offer. I didn't want to insult your sorry carcass by refusing."

"It was a real job offer." Joe climbed out of the fallen chair, righted it and sat down. "Our regular Santa has the flu." When he grinned, his full mustache hugged his mouth like an upside-down U. "Good to see you, buddy."

Sam shook his head and smiled. "Yeah, good to see you, too."

"Seriously," Joe said, "I know you're ticked, but you did a good job today. I hid behind the canned pears display and watched. You're good around kids. You want to do it again tomorrow?"

Sam grimaced. "I'd rather face a court-martial." Tossing a paper bag on the desk, he said, "Here. Some kid's mother actually made cookies for Santa. Can you believe that?"

"Yeah? What kind?" Joe reached for the bag. "My sisters always put a plate of oatmeal cookies and a glass of milk near the chimney on Christmas Eve." Humor pushed his cheeks into rosy apples. "I left M&M's. I didn't think he could get them at the North Pole."

"You're kidding."

"No. Didn't you ever do that when you were a kid?" Unrolling the top of the bag, he peered inside. "Don't tell me you didn't try to stay up all night to catch Santa when he came down the chimney, 'cause everyone I know did that."

"Sure. Of course."

Watching Joe inspect one of the large cookies Timmy's mother had made, Sam wondered why he'd just lied. He was not dishonest by nature, but suddenly he'd had such a strong image of Joe and his sisters secretly awaiting Santa's big entrance, of their parents peering in from a doorway, smiling in the background, that a myriad of confusing feelings rumbled through him—envy, regret and a strange, discomfiting inadequacy, ludicrous but powerful. Sam couldn't remember even believing in Santa Claus.

"Not bad." Joe nodded after taking a bite of cookie. "But we're running a special on iced molasses bars—one dozen for a dollar ninety-nine in the bakery. Now that's a good deal, my friend."

Sam frowned. "These are homemade," he said, incomprehensibly annoyed that Joe would compare store-bought to the cookies the redhead had made.

Joe shrugged. "You want homemade? My sister Carol is a whiz in the kitchen. She bakes all the time."

"Hmm."

"Carol's smart, too, and funny. You'd like her. Did I ever show you her picture?"

Sam quirked a brow at the man who had been his first friend way back in boot camp. "Are you trying to set me up with your sister?"

"Sure." Joe grinned. "That's what big brothers are for. Are you interested?"

Sam grew hot and prickly with the sudden urge to escape. He opened his mouth to decline, then closed it without speaking. He met Carol Lawson years ago and liked her. But she had Family written all over her even then, and Sam had the ethics not to start something he had no intention of finishing.

He shifted on the hard chair, both his leg and his conscience making him uncomfortable. If he was being honest with himself, he would have to admit that he'd come here looking for more than a job. He remembered the Lawson family, their boisterous meals, their easy way with one another, Joe's comfortable home.

Family.

He wanted to be around it. For awhile. But as a spectator, not a participant. He could close his eyes and imagine what it would be like to sit at a table that wasn't part of a mess hall. A small table, maybe, small enough to reach across and pour a drink for somebody else. Working together to set the places, smiling and laughing as you handed around the plates. There would be evidence of caring in the simplest ways. *Did you get enough potatoes?* Yeah. *Do you want more gravy?* Sure.

Looking out for each other. Appreciating that someone had bothered to make potatoes just because you liked them. Appreciating that someone *knew* you liked them.

Suddenly he wanted it so badly, he felt almost embarrassed, as if he'd been caught with his fly down. The muscles in his jaw tightened with resentment. He was like an ex-smoker who had to breathe the aroma from someone else's cigarette to get through the night. When he'd decided to come to Idaho, in the back of his mind had been the notion that he could be around Joe's family for a brief time and take the experience with him, like a secret, when he left—one final deep inhalation of someone else's smoke to store up for the years of deprivation that lay ahead.

Sam gave a sharp, reproachful shake of his head. The fact was, no matter how much he craved a glimpse of that life, he wasn't about to mislead anyone to get it.

To Joe he said, "I'm a bachelor. You know what they say about old dogs."

Joe grimaced. "Yeah, I know. I'm an old dog myself." Finishing the cookie, the big man brushed his hands. "Where are you staying tonight, Fido?"

"The Park Motel, outside of town."

"That dive? I wouldn't let my pet spider stay there."

With a brief smile, Sam said, "It's fine."

Joe pointed a finger. "You've been living with men too long. So listen, you'll come to dinner tonight. Tomorrow you can move your gear to the house. We have plenty of room."

Sam held up a hand. "Thanks, but I—"

"No, don't give me any crap." Pulling a piece of paper from the mess he called his in box, Joe muttered, "Besides, you'll be doing me a favor. My mother's all over me to get married. Give her someone new to torture." He grabbed a pen. "Here, I'll give you directions."

"Thanks, you've convinced me. I'll stay at the motel."

"What? Naw, seriously—"

"Seriously, Joe, I've got plans tonight. But soon." Sam reached for the bag of cookies, rolled the top of the paper sack and stood, relying on the cane more than he wanted to after a long day of sitting. And he did have plans. He just hadn't realized it until this moment.

Wanted, man to work on small organic farm...room, board... Plus, he amended silently, the kind of cookies Santa likes. And no strings.

All they wanted was a worker. Testing his bum leg, he decided that as a worker, he could come through just fine.

Rising, Joe held up a sheet of computer paper. "I had personnel print up a list of the jobs available in the store."

Leaning on his cane, Sam raised a brow. "What are they?"

Joe snapped the paper with a flourish, then cautioned, "Remember, this is only a preliminary list."

"Uh-huh. Is there anything on that page that involves wearing a giant crow costume and waving people into your parking lot?"

Eyes widening, Joe lowered the list. "That's not a bad idea. Not a crow, though. What's that Froot Loops bird?" He fished around for a pad of paper. "We could do a tie-in with breakfast cereals. Sugar-sweet savings. How does that sound? I— Hey, where're you goin'?"

"Get the elf to do it. She'd make a great bird." Sam tossed the words over his shoulder on his way to the door. He knew where he was headed. "I'll call you tomorrow."

"What about dinner?"

Raising the bag of cookies, Sam smiled. "All I need is a quart of milk. I'll call you."

"You're going to break my sister's heart?" Joe put a hand over his chest.

Grasping the office doorknob, Sam paused long enough to answer. "No. I'm not going to break anyone's heart."

Moving carefully, Dani lifted a steaming apple-raisin pie from the oven. She could feel the heat of the deep-dish Pyrex through her oven mitts and saw that some of the juice was still bubbling up through the heart-shaped vent she'd cut into the crust.

Setting pie number twelve atop a baking rack on the crowded counter, she tallied her creations—four apple-raisin, two cranberry-pear and six pumpkin pies, dozens of cookies, cooled and ready for boxing, in five varieties—molasses-ginger, milk chocolate chip, honey-nut peanut butter, the oatmeal-coconut crunch she'd given Timmy yesterday for Santa Claus, and the buttery Russian tea balls that sold so well around the holidays.

Sweet Dreams, the baking business she ran to earn extra money during the winter, was doing surprisingly well for a home business, but she was pooped. She'd been baking since four this morning. It was now one in the afternoon, and she still had a half dozen sour cream banana breads and her popular cinnamon-streusal orange coffee cake to go.

She would be up most of the night tonight, baking and packaging, but Pop would make the deliveries for her tomorrow and Timmy would be in school, so perhaps she'd grab a nap then.

Closing the oven door, Dani decided to give the reliable old workhorse a twenty-minute breather while she sat down with a cup of coffee. It was warm in the kitchen, pleasantly so, given the chill outside. Pouring a mug of coffee from the pot she'd been nursing all day, Dani felt her stomach contract with hunger.

Bypassing the fresh cookies that represented her profits, she helped herself to one of the giant oatmeal-coconut crunch cookies she'd made yesterday and plunked herself into a chair at the table. Every muscle in her shoulders and back groaned in protest at the change in position, but her legs, relieved of the pressure from standing so many hours, thanked her.

Working so hard made her body feel old before its time, but in some ways she didn't care. She was working for her son, so a sore muscle was no more resented than one of the permanent silvery stretch marks she'd acquired during her pregnancy.

These things—sore muscles, stretch marks—were just battle scars. As long as she won the war, who cared if she emerged a bit dog-eared? And the war in this case was raising a happy, well-adjusted child on her own.

Taking Timmy to see Santa yesterday had made her aware all over again how lucky she was. Watching her little boy poke at Santa's white beard, seeing him politely hand over the cookies he'd asked her to bake, her heart had swelled with love. How could a father not want to be there? She would never understand it, not if she lived to be a hundred, not if she had twelve more children!

Obviously Brian had regretted his relationship with her, but that shouldn't have precluded a relationship with his child. Her ex-Mr. Right hadn't cared about either of them. He'd never even seen his son.

Timmy had an eager little heart and arms that hugged like nobody's business. He deserved so much more than a father who was nothing but a name.

Dunking the cookie into her coffee, Dani took a careful bite.

Pop had dropped her ad off at the newspaper office yesterday. She'd experienced a few trickles of anxiety since then over what she was about to do, but she wouldn't let fear stop her. Placing that ad gave her hope. It gave her a chance, at least, to ensure that the next time her son wanted a daddy's kiss, it wouldn't have to come from a toy father.

She glanced out the window, where the world seemed to be moored permanently in winter. Somewhere out there was a man who knew how to love a little boy, how to make him feel special and safe and strong in his own right. A man whose hugs were given free.

Just one decent man with the heart to stick around. That's all she needed.

And who cared if they never had a lot of money? If she had to, she would work hard every day of her life. As long as he pulled his own weight, fine.

She doubted he'd be especially handsome, but that was okay, too. Timmy's father had been ambitious, smart and charming. Especially charming. His attention had made her feel special. Being in a relationship with him had made her feel...

So alone she'd thought she might die.

She and Brian—and this had occurred to her only recently—had never really *talked,* not about anything important. She had tried too hard to please him, terrified of rocking the boat, shutting her eyes to the fact that it was already sinking. Then she'd gotten pregnant, and Brian had jumped ship.

Now she knew she would never again beg for a man's attention, and she would never, ever let anyone hurt Timmy. When she chose a man to join their lives—*if* she did—it would be someone who needed and wanted them as much as they wanted him.

The peal of the phone jolted Dani to attention. Break time was over. Finishing the cookie, she crossed the kitchen and grabbed the receiver before the machine could pick up. "H'lo?"

"Hello. May I speak with Gene, please?"

"He's not—" She covered the mouthpiece, finished chewing and swallowed. "Excuse me. He's not here right now. May I take a message?"

There was a pause during which Dani brushed her fingers on her apron, plucked a pen from the cup next to the phone and held it over the scratch pad, waiting.

The next time the deep voice rumbled, she leaned on her elbow and just listened.

"I'm calling in regard to the position you have open. My name is Sam Mclean."

The voice on the other end of the line was measured, rich as a truffle, smooth as caramel.

"Position?"

"A want ad was posted—"

"Want ad? Oh!" Dani straightened, her attention sharpening. Good heavens! Had the ad appeared in the Sunday paper already? Pop had only dropped it off yesterday. She'd expected to have several days, a week....

"You, um, asked for my father?"

"If your father's name is Gene."

She frowned. "The notice gave his name?"

"Yes, ma'am."

Yes, ma'am. He said it politely, automatically, in a voice comfortable showing respect.

Dani clutched the phone in a death grip, using her other hand to draw dozens of tiny boxes on the pad in front of her. He was calling about *that* ad, but why had the paper listed Pop? Someone must have messed up and used the name of the person who dropped the materials off, or...

Or her father had deliberately used his name so he could screen prospective sons-in-law himself. *Pop!* she groused silently, *I'm not a little girl anymore.*

Taking a breath, Dani spoke with all the authority and confidence she could muster.

"*I* placed the ad, Mr.—"

"Mclean. Sam."

"Sam. I'm doing the—" she couldn't call it hiring "—interviewing."

Another pause, more brief this time. "I'm sorry, ma'am, I didn't catch your name."

"Oh, forgive me. It's Dani. Dani Harmon."

"I'd like an interview, Ms. Harmon. That is, if you're agreeable."

Such a reverently polite tone. Dani twined the telephone cord around her fingers. Was she agreeable? She longed to rely on her instincts, but instinct was a hard thing to trust when you had no track record. And this was happening so quickly!

Taking a deep breath, she closed her eyes, crossed her fingers and prayed for intuition. "I'm agreeable," she said after a protracted moment.

"Good. I realize it's Sunday, but I'm free today if—"

"Today?"

Swiftly, she scanned the kitchen. Every inch of available counter space was covered with pies, cookies, pans and utensils. Glancing at herself, Dani realized she wasn't in much better shape than her kitchen. Jeans, an old fuzzy sweater, her hair pulled back in a riotous ponytail—the editors of *Cosmo* would never approve.

On the other hand...

A candidate for husband and father might as well see right up front what he was getting. This was a working kitchen, and she was a working mom. Back in the days when she'd been a well-paid legal secretary in Los Angeles, she would have worn a skirt and heels for a daytime appointment, silk pants and sandals for evening. Now she was a twenty-eight-year-old single mother with a cesarean scar hiding beneath her jeans and no time for makeup. The last time she had used mascara, it was to fill in a chip on her coffee table.

So she had a choice. She could either put Sam Mclean off until tomorrow, scour the house, run out to buy a tube of lipstick and pretend she was Jane Seymour—*Who, me, perspire? It was only twins*— or she could spin the wheel and land on What You See Is What You Get.

Adrenaline pumped as she made her decision. "Today is fine, Mr. Mclean. How does three o'clock sound?"

"Three o'clock," he said in his calm, soothing tone, "that sounds like a good time for an interview."

The road to Dani Harmon's farm was gravel-paved, potholed and about to ruin the new shocks on Sam's Buick.

He peered through the windshield at the winter-gray afternoon, steering the car slowly along the gravel and snow. The directions she'd given him were clear, but he checked them again anyway as he approached 2140 Longacre Road.

This was it, all right. Instead of being glad he'd come the right way, however, Sam frowned. It was hard to reconcile this ramshackle place with the picture he'd formed in his head.

Somehow, he had expected the redhead and her son to reside in a gingerbread cottage, well-cared-for and comfortable and redolent of family. The house Sam looked at suggested hard times. The siding was weathered, a rain gutter was down and as he stopped the car, he got a good look at a roof that needed a patch job soon if it was going to shelter the family adequately through winter.

And yet despite the obvious disrepair, Sam saw evidence of a woman's touch everywhere he looked.

Like makeup on an aged face, ruffled curtains dressed the sagging windows. An ornamental wreath with pine cones, plastic holly berries and a big, happy bow graced the door, and suspended from the porch eaves, a wooden carving of a cow, a pig and a bird standing on each other's backs bore the message Welcome, friends.

I like it, Sam thought, liking it all the more because he saw right away that he could fix the broken spindle in the porch railing and repair the rain gutter.

He wasn't sure whether he was here under false pretenses or not. She was looking for an employee. Working and residing on a run-down farm in Idaho had never been part of his life plan. On the other hand...

"I don't have a life plan anymore," Sam muttered as he got out of the car. It required only a glance at the cane resting against the front passenger seat for Sam to decide he would leave it right where it was. Sheer vanity, sure, but he didn't care. Rolling his shoulders inside the leather bomber jacket, he adjusted his tie. He hadn't had a job interview in years.

After so long knowing exactly what his purpose was, what he would be doing a week, two months, a year from now, it was hell to find himself suddenly aimless. Mornings were the worst. From his first cup of watery coffee to the last bite of rubber eggs and toy sausages he purchased at whatever fast-food establishment happened to be near, Sam felt his purposelessness like a weight around his neck.

His shoes ground the snow and gravel on the way to the house, and he felt a curious heat in his veins—anticipation, a sensation he hadn't had in some time. Rather than speeding up, he slowed his steps, an unconscious effort to make the feeling last.

Controlling his limp as best he could, he walked up the porch steps, listening to the wood creak and thinking, *I could fix that, too.*

He smiled as he passed the whimsical welcome sign. Dani Harmon had a job proposition, and darned if he wasn't eager to discuss it.

His heart pumped in earnest as he knocked on the door.

Inside the house, Dani's palm started to sweat the moment she reached for the knob. Her body revved like a car with the accelerator pressed to the floor. She hadn't felt this nervous since her junior high school prom. She hadn't dated anyone since before Timmy was born.

Taking a deep breath, she steadied her nerves, said

a quick silent prayer that this wouldn't turn out to be the biggest mistake of her life, and opened the door.

Holy moly.

She forgot to say hello. She forgot to introduce herself.

In the hour and a half since his call, Dani had been wondering what Sam Mclean looked like. She wasn't expecting Mel Gibson, of course. The Mel Gibsons of the world did not answer personal ads.

The Harrison Fords, however, apparently did.

Fortunately, divinity—or vanity—had overruled her earlier decision to let it all hang out, and she'd changed into charcoal trousers and a delicately woven sweater in palest pearl gray. Her hair, free from its customary ponytail, was loose and curling, caught on one side with a barrette. She'd even managed a swipe of lip gloss. When the temptation to scrounge up some old eyeshadow had reared its head, however, she'd drawn the line.

"Ms. Harmon?" His voice sounded as rich and sonorous as it had on the phone. "I'm Sam."

He held out his hand, and Dani hesitated only a moment before accepting it.

"Sam!" His name flew from her lips on a puff of breath that was impossibly girlish. In an attempt to recover her demeanor, she nodded brusquely. "Well. You're on time." *Nice save,* she congratulated herself, cringing at the rapid shift from Betty Boop to Nurse Ratchet.

Long, tanned fingers closed around hers.

Pop, a door-to-door salesman for thirty years, had taught her that a handshake could tell a lot about a person. This one did. Sam's palm was warm despite the cold weather, tough but not callused. She knew immediately that he hadn't worked on a farm in a long while, if ever.

As for his grip, it was firm enough to command respect, gentle enough to communicate his awareness of her as a woman. The release was neat and quick, making the contact seem casual. But a handshake was a two-way street. What she learned about herself was even more telling than what she gleaned about Sam.

The moment their palms slid together, Dani felt a surge of electricity that made her whole torso tingle. If after almost six years of celibacy she thought she was immune to a man's touch, well then, she was full of beans.

Dropping her arm to her side the instant he let go, Dani curled her fingers into her palm. "Please, come in." She stepped back, allowing him to pass.

Sam Mclean was wearing a leather bomber jacket that, if not new, was nonetheless of good quality. From his well-pressed trousers to his neatly trimmed brown hair, to the look of intelligent awareness in his hazel eyes, there seemed to be endless clues suggesting that dire financial straits were not the reason he'd answered her ad.

He was handsome, tall and had a voice like melting butter. Surely he didn't need to find a woman through the classifieds.

Suddenly the recklessness of what she was doing hit her like a blow from a hammer. This was a stranger. A tall, male, strong-looking stranger.

She'd been living in small towns too long! Tall at five feet seven inches, she was certainly no weakling, but it occurred to her that she'd been expecting applicants who hadn't had a good meal in a long while, down-and-outers whose reasons for responding to her ad would be evident. And she had not meant to have anyone over until after she had checked their references, personal and otherwise. Then she'd heard Sam Mclean's voice and...

Her hand tightened on the doorknob.

She'd been in control of her life, in control of herself, for years. Now she'd invited a man into her home and just one look at him—one handshake—made hope stir in her breast...where it didn't belong.

Sam took the single step up and into the house. With a nod, he crossed past her into the living room, glanced at the worn sofa, at a finger painting Timmy had left on the coffee table, and at the dining room table covered with jars of homemade preserves, cakes and other sweets ready for packaging. And then he did the oddest thing.

Standing where he was, half turned from her, his hands in his pockets, Sam closed his eyes for a moment...and inhaled. Simply inhaled, slowly, single-mindedly, as if the deep breath was a meditation.

Bemused, Dani frowned until she realized what he was smelling. Her chocolate chip turnovers were still in the oven. The rich, sweet aroma filled the small house.

Letting his eyes flicker open, Sam turned to her. His mouth rose on one side.

Dani stood with the door open, allowing cold air to chill the living room. She had almost convinced herself not to close the door at all, keeping clear a path of rapid escape should he turn out to be a fruit-cake.

But he didn't seem like a fruitcake.

She had never seen a smile like his before, didn't know how to read it. There was admiration in the tilt of his lips, a compliment, but sadness and something more, too...wistfulness.

It surprised her. Wistful was not an expression she would have expected to see on such a strong, virile face. She didn't know what to make of it. Or of him.

And then his stomach growled. Loudly.

Sam's eyes flared briefly. His expression changed to one Dani could read easily—utter embarrassment.

That's when she decided to trust him.

"I haven't had lunch, either." She smiled.

And shut the door.

Chapter Four

"I'll get that for you, ma'am."

Lifting a rack of cooled cookies off the crowded kitchen counter, Sam cleared a space for the tray Dani pulled from the oven. When she crossed in front of him, Sam wasn't sure which aroma he liked more—the sweet scent of lilac that wafted from her hair or the chocolate, butter and cinnamon that had him practically groaning with hunger.

Damn his talkative stomach! The last thing he wanted was for Dani Harmon to think he was desperate for this job. He could have had lunch this afternoon. Money wasn't an issue. But having suffered through numerous fast-food meals over the past few days, he didn't want even one more bite of anything that came wrapped in paper. Eating alone at a coffee shop counter didn't hold much appeal, either, so he'd passed on the midday meal today.

Depositing a tray of buttery, rich-smelling pastries

on the counter, Dani turned toward the refrigerator.
Sam watched her reach up, removing boxes of cereal,
and couldn't help his reaction.

As she stretched, her short sweater pulled up, re-
vealing a glimpse of taut stomach. Sam felt his hunger move from his stomach to…lower. He tried not
to stare at her as she turned to take the tray from his
hands.

"I'll do it," he said hoarsely. *Get a grip, man.*

Quickly, he placed the tray atop the old refrigerator and stepped back. Time to get down to business.

Standing in her kitchen, he could almost forget the
long years of eating in mess halls and diners.

"Maybe we should do the interview first, ma'am.
Before lunch." Dani looked surprised, but he per-
sisted, feeling a need to get down to business. "If
you have an application, I could fill it out."

"An application?"

"I don't have a résumé. Sorry, but I've been in
the Army for a dozen years." He shrugged. "I
haven't needed a résumé."

Dani's eyes widened. "Well, I, uh, I didn't expect…" She frowned. "I don't think I need a résumé. A couple of personal references, perhaps."

"That's no problem."

She nodded slowly. How did a man make the tran-
sition from the Army to personal ads?

"I loved *M*A*S*H*," she murmured. The moment
the stupid words left her mouth, she blushed. "It's
all I know about the Army, I mean."

He smiled and Dani felt like the swirl in her butter-
scotch bundt cake—warm and melty and sweet.

His gaze seemed direct, devoid of the attempt to

charm. She couldn't claim to be a sterling judge of character, not after Brian, but Sam Mclean seemed genuine, and she liked that. She liked it a lot.

"Please, sit down." Gesturing to the kitchen table, Dani offered him a hastily assembled plate of cookies when they were both seated. "I have plenty."

He smiled at the understatement. "I've tasted your cookies before."

"You have? Where?"

"Lawson's."

"I don't sell my products at Lawson's. They have their own bakery."

"I know. The cookies were a gift from your son. I was Lawson's Santa yesterday."

Dani opened her eyes wide. "That was you?" The Santa who had taken so much time with her son? Timmy had chattered about his visit with Santa for half the afternoon.

"I was helping out a friend," Sam said dismissively, shaking his head. "I'm afraid I wasn't very good at playing St. Nick."

"Oh, no, you were wonderful!" The energetic affirmation surprised them both. In her mind's eye, Dani saw him again, listening intently to her son, patting the small knees gently with gloved hands.

Her gaze dropped shyly to the table.

Where had this man come from? He was gentle with children, his voice could melt butter, and he was good-looking enough to make her forget why she'd placed the ad in the first place.

Dani took a deep breath. She hadn't had so much as a date since her third month of pregnancy, and that was almost six years ago. She hadn't *wanted* a date since then. Brian's desertion had brought all her hidden fears roaring to life. She wasn't pretty enough, smart enough, special enough. She'd never hold anyone's attention for long....

"You have a fine son."

Dani raised her head and saw admiration in Sam's eyes. Praise for a job well done. Oh, boy. A woman's doubts and fears could melt away under such a gaze.

"Thank you." She tempered gratitude with all the poise she could muster. "My son means the world to me."

"That's how it should be."

Running a fingertip along the edge of the table, Dani moistened her dry lips. "I'm glad you think so. That's why I'm doing this. Placing an ad, I mean." Smiling, she rolled her eyes self-consciously. "An ad! I can't even believe... I've never done anything like this before."

"Seems like a reasonable thing to do."

"Does it?" She gave a doubtful laugh. "Really?"

He shrugged. "Isn't that how most people go about it?"

Pushing at the curls that sprang stubbornly around her temples no matter how tightly she slicked back her hair, Dani leaned on an elbow. She was fluttery inside, as eager to please and impress as a girl on her first date.

"Oh, boy." She pressed a hand to her forehead. "This is not how I thought it would be. I mean, I wouldn't normally go about it at all. You know?"

Shaking his head slowly, Sam narrowed his eyes. "No, I'm afraid not." Unable to wait any longer, he reached for the plate of cookies, offering them to Dani before he chose one for himself.

Breaking her cookie in half, Dani reflected on what a simple gesture that was, offering someone else food before you took any yourself. A common courtesy. Except in her experience, courtesy wasn't common at all.

In small but powerful ways, Sam Mclean exhibited decency. As if he was from another time, he made civility a priority.

Hope puddled in Dani's heart. She was a realist, had been for years. But deep, deep down, romance still whispered, and she knew that if she let it, her imagination would spin straw into gold.

Her personal ad had been a statement as much as anything else—*I, Danielle Lynn Harmon, single mother and struggling working woman, do hereby acknowledge that marriage is a contract and that the head is the only part of the human body qualified to choose a mate.*

But that wasn't the way she wanted it to be, and Sam Mclean reminded her with attentive hazel eyes, a slow wry smile and a bourbon voice that she was not as immune to a man's appeal as she ought to be. Not by a long shot.

In answer to his question, she said, "I didn't think I'd be in this position. I never thought I'd have the need...or even the desire to— Some of my friends placed ads of a sort in L.A.—that's where we're from—but even then it never crossed my mind. I never even came close."

Her bumbling elaboration must have confused

him, because he narrowed his eyes to a squint. "Did you have your own business in Los Angeles?"

"No."

His gaze flicked meaningfully around the kitchen. Clearly, he recognized the amount of work the baked goods represented. "Have you been working by yourself here?"

"Pop—my father—helps where he can. We don't do much farming in the winter. That's why I'd like to build a greenhouse. I supplement my income by selling my desserts and the jams and preserves I can in the fall."

He smiled that sleepy, liquid half-smile, and Dani had to force herself not to wiggle in her chair. She felt like someone was practicing high dives in her stomach.

"I don't think I've ever met a woman who did her own canning."

"Well, if you'd met me a few years ago, you still wouldn't have." When he arched a brow, she explained, "I moved here with my father and son from California. Los Angeles. I worked in an office full time and bought jam in the grocery store and cakes at the bakery."

"Quite a leap from L.A. to Idaho."

"In more ways than one," she agreed. "It's quite a leap from being an officer in the Army to living on an organic fruit and vegetable farm, too. A barely surviving organic farm." He might as well know their financial position right up front.

Sam both responded to her observation and acknowledged the information with a slow nod.

Pleating one of the paper napkins she'd set on the

table with the cookies, Dani said softly, "I wanted a different kind of life for my son. That's why I'm here." She raised her eyes from the napkin to Sam and smiled. "What's your excuse?"

The baldly stated question signaled a conversational shift. *Time for the interview portion of our program.* Dani tried to appear casual as she waited for a response, but she knew his answer was important. If he said he'd been court-martialed for selling government-owned weapons to minors, for example, this meeting would be adjourned. And she didn't want that. In fact, when she realized she was holding her breath, she knew she wanted very much for this meeting to go on.

Sam chewed and swallowed a large bite of cookie. He picked up a napkin, wiped the crumbs from his hands and said, "Beats the hell out of me."

Dani blinked.

"I don't have a plan." Sam spared her the need of asking him to elaborate. "I was in an accident. I'm still in one piece, but I won't be leading any training marches, and that's what I was good at."

Dani could not miss the air of finality in his tone or the tightness around his lips.

"I have a friend," Sam continued, "in Idaho. He owns Lawson's."

"And you were helping him out by playing Santa?"

"Mmm." He let drop the subject of his stint as St. Nick. "Your ad specified references. I have those for you, if you don't mind making a long distance call."

"I don't mind," Dani murmured. There was

much, much more she wanted to know, about the Army, his accident, his injury, but clearly these were topics he did not wish to discuss, and she supposed she didn't have to know more about his Army days in order to make her decision. Sticking to what she considered the essentials, she asked, "Do you have family in Idaho?"

"No."

"But you'd be willing to settle here?"

"If everything works out. If it doesn't work out, there's a desk job waiting. In the ad, you mentioned a trial period."

"Yes." Dani nodded vigorously. "I thought that would be best in case we don't..." Her hand stirred the air. "I mean, we might not... You could decide you don't like it here."

Sam glanced around the homey kitchen, cluttered with her creations. His features relaxed and softened. Then he glanced at her, and his expression altered again, in a way she couldn't define.

There was something mysterious and unspoken in Sam's gaze, something that made the flesh on Dani's arms and legs tingle. He looked at her the way a man looked at a woman in whom he took more than a passing interest. It had been a long time since a man had looked at her that way, even longer since she'd welcomed it. Still, when he spoke, his voice and his eyes were direct and devoid of flirtation.

"I like it so far."

Like snow in spring, doubt melted and Dani felt warm for the first time in...forever. All from a stranger's words.

Surely no one should have that much power, she thought. And yet...

Oh, it felt good! It was good to feel a blush coming on, to know that if she spoke, she would stammer because every nerve tingled with awareness. It felt utterly delicious to hope again, like a young girl.

It was crazy. It was foolish and reckless.

He'd answered an ad asking for a husband. What kind of man would do such a thing?

What kind of woman would place the ad?

Dani looked across the table.

He has secrets, she speculated, *but nothing bad. And, after all, I have a few of my own.*

What kind of man would answer an ad asking for a husband, and what kind of woman would place one? Maybe, just maybe, the kind of man and woman who were crazy, foolish and reckless enough to make this thing work.

Dani tried once more to remind herself she was doing this only for Timmy. But when Fate dropped a present in your lap, it would be rude not to open it. For years, she had suppressed longings that would, when dashed, only bring pain. Now images of the life she had once dreamed about popped and sparkled in her head. Laughter, belonging, togetherness...and long sultry nights—for a few exhilarating moments, her imagination ran gloriously, wickedly free.

"I'd like to think I could be of some help to you, Dani." Sam's sure, quiet voice reminded her they had come to no decisions yet. "But the truth is, I don't have much experience in this area."

Dani felt her brows rise involuntarily. *He's talking about marriage,* she reminded herself, embarrassed when she realized her thoughts had been running along more primitive lines.

Pleased and a trifle amused by his total lack of male arrogance, she smiled. "Neither have I." She shrugged. "Maybe it's better that way. Fewer expectations, you know?"

Sam frowned. "You *should* have expectations. This is your life, your livelihood." He sounded almost protective of her, and again Dani felt an upsurge of hope. "What's my job description?"

"Job description? Well, I— Uh..." Putting a hand to her temple, Dani lowered her gaze to the table and shook her head. "That's a funny way to put it," she muttered.

"You must have some idea of what my duties will be."

"Duties?" Perhaps it was his military background, but Sam's choice of words suddenly left a lot to be desired.

"These are things you should be prepared to discuss with everyone who answers your ad."

"I should discuss 'duties'?"

Obviously disturbed by the ironic spin she put on the word, Sam clasped his hands on the table. "Maybe you should have your father—what's his name?"

"Gene."

"Gene." Sam nodded, musing. "It might be a good idea to have him along to conduct these interviews with you."

Dani's mouth dropped open like a pelican at a fish fry. "Have my *father* along?"

A slow, seeping stiffness—like rigor mortis—crept

through her. She should have known it was too good to be true. The man's first fatal flaw had reared its head—paternalism, a blatant lack of faith in a woman's ability to govern her life.

Hoping she was wrong, Dani probed lightly. "Why would I want to do that? This is my decision, and a very personal one at that."

Sam nodded, easily agreeing. "Absolutely. And a very important one. That's why you can't afford to let just any man off the street come in here and convince you he's up to the task. If you don't tell him what's expected of him and watch his reaction, how will you know if he can perform when push comes to shove?"

Dani was speechless.

Perform?

"Look," Sam added, resting his elbows on the table, his smile once more gentle and beguiling, "all I'm saying is that from the looks of things, you can't afford to lose any more time."

Oh!

A tide of embarrassment, red-hot and furious, filled Dani from her head to her toes. What the devil had she been thinking when she placed that asinine ad? Being single was infinitely preferable to having some stranger insult her in her own home.

Pushing herself to a standing position, she placed her palms on the table and glared.

Sam watched the woman rise like a chorus of Greek furies. Emotion trembled through her long, slender limbs. Her jaw tensed, and her pale skin flushed to a shade almost as intense as her curly red hair. What had he said to warrant this reaction?

They'd been getting along great—too well, in fact. Everything about her was appealing to the point of distraction. Her softness, her earthiness, the way she exuded strength one minute and shyness the next. She had a voice that made him think of honey on warm toast.

He'd been ready to tell her he'd worked on a dozen organic farms, had years of experience, was the answer to her prayers. Most men, he suspected, would have the same reaction. When he thought about it, it was a bad idea all around for Dani Harmon to conduct these interviews on her own. At the very least, whoever applied should be made aware that there damn well was a man around the place— a protective father, Sam hoped—someone to make sure that whoever took the job would keep his mind on pruning fruit trees or whatever it was you did to a fruit tree.

Further, an interviewer had to be tough, unemotional. If the applicant couldn't do the job, then— phht!—outta there. Dani Harmon was too damn nice. Making Santa Claus cookies, offering lunch because she heard his stomach growl—before they'd said five words to each other. He could tell already she wouldn't be able to oust an ant from a picnic.

"How *dare* you?" The voice that carried across the table sounded less like honey and more like molten lava. Sam frowned and rose to face her. He felt the surprise on his brow.

"Get out." Her hand shook as she pointed to the kitchen door. "For your information, I did not place that ad looking for some sort of stud service! I placed the ad for my son. *For my son,* is that clear?" She dropped her hand and lifted her chin. "Speaking for myself, I am perfectly content to remain exactly as I am. In fact, now that I've had time to reconsider, I'm quite sure I was temporarily insane when I placed that ad. And may I say on behalf of all women over the age of twelve, your implication that I am somehow over the hill is offensive not only to me but to anyone who has ever had to fight sexism or age bias in America. So—" pausing for breath, Dani drew herself up "—in your ear, bucko."

"Mommy, are you angry?"

Whipping around, Dani was aghast when she saw her son and her father hovering in the kitchen doorway. With his gloved hands on the little boy's shoulders, Gene looked from Dani to the stranger in their kitchen, his eyebrows rising like clouds above the frames of his glasses.

"How long have you been standing there?" Her voice emerged half rasp, half whisper.

A tiny smile flicked at the corner of Gene's mouth. He stroked his chin. "Huh, let's see. Must've come in right about the time you started talking about horses. Heard you say something about a stud service."

"Are we getting a horse, Mommy? Oh, boy!"

Timmy started jumping up and down. Dani proceeded quickly to her son, turning him around and nudging him gently but firmly out of the kitchen. "Let's get your coat and mittens off," she mumbled.

Sam looked on in utter consternation. What in hell just happened?

The other man, Gene, glanced after his daughter and grandson with a bland smile on his friendly face.

From the living room, they heard Timmy alternating between gleeful chants. "A horse! A horse! In your ear, bucko!"

Dani shushed him as they retreated to another part of the house.

Turning, the bespectacled man glanced with interest at the plate of cookies sitting on the table. He looked at Sam. "You want some coffee to go with that, son?"

Chapter Five

"So he left then? Just like that?"

Dani sat at her kitchen table, pretending an interest in the lasagna her father had brought home from the church potluck. Timmy was singing along with an *Aladdin* tape, so she didn't have to worry about his overhearing—a small comfort in what was turning out to be a series of humiliations.

After ushering Timmy to his room earlier, explaining that "in your ear" was not to be repeated and agreeing to give herself a time-out for using bad language, Dani had returned to the kitchen to find her father sipping coffee at the table. Alone.

Gene had doffed his heavy coat and earmuffs, but now he wore a troubled frown that appeared almost as heavy as the discarded garments.

"He left after I explained things," Pop said.

Dani shrugged, chewing a piece of sausage as if she took more interest in Lolly Thorton's lasagna recipe than she did in what had recently transpired in her own kitchen.

In truth, her embarrassment was so huge, so choking, she wasn't sure she'd be able to swallow a bite.

Her father had explained everything.

Apparently Gene had been so uncomfortable with Dani's decision to advertise for a husband, so certain she would wind up with, as he put it, "the runt of the litter," that he'd decided to help her out by advertising for a hired hand. His reasoning—honest, upstanding men answered ads for work while only a gigolo would respond to an ad for a husband.

Dani forced herself to swallow the piece of lasagna she'd been chewing for the past two minutes, then set her fork on the plate, abandoning all pretense of eating. Pop was blinking rapidly behind his glasses, looking as sad and worried as a puppy who'd been caught teething on the remote control. Dani didn't have the heart to be upset with him. He'd merely been trying to protect a grown-up daughter, and that was an awkward occupation, at best.

She wanted to get up, put her arms around him and tell him she understood, but her heart was too burdened. She couldn't make herself move.

"He figured it'd be best if he left," her father offered into the silence. "He didn't want you to be embarrassed, I think. Not that you have anything to be embarrassed about. The whole thing is my fault, honey."

"Pop—"

"It is. I didn't think anyone would call so soon, and I figured I'd be here when they did call, and— Aw, hell, I don't know what I figured."

Sure you do, Dani thought. *You figured some nice single man would take one look at this farm and one look at me, and it would be love at first sight. You figured a nice man like Sam would see all that you see in me.*

And Sam *was* a nice man, Dani acknowledged, realizing she'd misconstrued most of what he'd said this afternoon. He'd come for a job, and when she'd failed to protect her own interests by interviewing him properly he had simply tried to give her advice. *Fundamental protective instincts,* she thought. *Not a bad quality.*

While Pop nursed his coffee, Dani sat stiffly erect, nursing her wounded pride.

She knew she should be glad Sam Mclean left when he did. He'd spared them both the embarrassment of acknowledging her real intent here today, to snag a husband.

What had she been thinking? She hadn't placed the ad solely for Timmy's sake. She grasped the truth now with grim, unavoidable clarity. Sam had brought the realization sharply to life.

All it had taken were a few moments in his company to give Dani's sluggish imagination enough material to weave dozens of daydreams, all beginning and ending with the same theme—family. Never again would she be able to convince herself that she wanted a husband solely for the sake of her son.

"Are you upset that he didn't stay?" Gene's question was tentative and uneasy.

Forcing herself to relax, Dani met her father's gaze with a wry smile. "Am I upset he wasn't applying for the husband position, you mean?" Her heart broke a bit at the expression of sheer pain that crossed Gene's face. "No, I'm not upset. Why should I be? That was the dumbest idea I ever had."

Reaching deep inside for a self-mocking chuckle, she shook her head. "I think I had a temporary brain freeze. You know one really good thing that came out of this, Pop?" Dani rose with her plate and the half-full pan of lasagna Gene had brought home. "I realized I can't sacrifice my happiness for my son's. Maybe that sounds selfish."

The dish clattered as she set it in the sink. She turned on the faucet and water came out in belching, half-frozen bursts. "I know how badly Timmy wants a daddy, but I don't want a husband. I figured that out for sure. I really don't."

"Aw, honey—"

Dani pulled a roll of aluminum foil out of a drawer and ripped off a large sheet. "You want me to leave this lasagna out for later, Pop? Do you think you'll get hungry again?"

"He said to tell you thanks for the cookie. And he said he was sorry for the mix-up."

With brisk, efficient movements, Dani covered the pan of lasagna, the aroma of tomato and spices making her almost queasy—but not as queasy as her father's next words did.

"I think he liked you."

Glass jars rattled when Dani shut the refrigerator door. "I'm going to walk the driveway, see if we need to lay more salt." This time the smile she mustered for her pop came and went faster than a shooting star.

Pausing at the coat tree only long enough to grab

a bulky jacket with mittens stuffed in the pockets and a heavy knit cap, which she scrunched on her head, Dani let herself out of the house and started walking down the long, straight driveway.

Snow and rock salt ground beneath her feet. For a long, satisfying while all she heard was the crunch, crunch, crunch of her steps on the drive.

Striding rapidly, Dani was about a quarter mile away from the house before she tasted the tears sliding silently down her face.

She came to a halt, mittened fists bunched at her sides. *Damn, damn damn!* She'd let down her defenses, and it hadn't taken long at all to start wishing again. Daydreams—she hated them. What was the point of wanting, always wanting, when the something you wanted stayed forever out of reach? It hurt, and Dani was through hurting for this lifetime.

Darn him...darn Sam Mclean. Darn all men who spoke little but made promises with their eyes.

The way he'd looked at her, she'd thought...

Releasing a sigh as harsh and ragged as the winter-bare trees, Dani gazed straight ahead. She didn't see the road or her tumbledown farm. Rather, she imagined a man and woman standing together in the doorway of a home bright with fresh white paint, decorated with Christmas lights. The husband and wife grinned as they watched a young boy and girl throw their first snowballs of the season. Laughter erupted in joyous bursts, splattering like a snowball in the cold winter air.

Sighing, Dani wiped a mitten-clad finger beneath her eyes, then stuck her hands in her pockets and gave a great, philosophical sigh. Life was funny.

Some people dreamed so big—movie stardom, Olympic medals, running a country—and against the odds, they accomplished their goals.

Then there were people like her, normal people with normal dreams, nothing extraordinary, nothing terribly grand, and yet as out of reach as a walk on the moon. Why was that? Why had her fondest dreams always seemed like a mirage, appearing clear and real until she reached out to grab them and her hand closed around nothing?

Her problems with relationships had begun in the first grade. Every day after school, Dani and three of her friends had played house. Relishing the idea of being a homemaker even then, Dani had loved playing the mother, until one day out of the clear blue Sheldon Abels, who'd played the father, callously threw her over for the "wife" in the "house" next door.

Dani kicked at a clump of icy gravel.

The problem with Sam Mclean was that he was quiet. Mystery lurked in the eyes of quiet men, and to a lonely woman, mystery equaled promise.

But I'm not lonely, she contradicted her own thoughts.

Sniffling as she wiped a woolly mitten beneath her nose, she looked toward her little house. She had Pop, she had Timmy. She wasn't lonely now. But she had been as an only child—especially after her mother died and Pop immersed himself in work, trying vainly to bury the pain.

Dani frowned. Now she worked nine, often ten or more hours herself, sometimes six days a week.

Would Timmy look back someday and wonder what he'd missed?

Was he growing up secretly scared and uncertain, as she had?

How she longed to talk it over with someone, especially late at night when worries whispered loudest. To have the luxury of someone else's ear, someone else's confidence. But she didn't want to burden Pop. He still carried the guilt of his own parenting difficulties.

Turning toward the road, Dani plunged her hands into her deep pockets, expelled a long, icy cold breath and resumed walking, slowly.

The feminists of the world might never forgive her saying so, but there were times when single seemed like a decidedly unnatural state of being.

There were times lately when Sam wondered if an alien force had taken control of his mind, times—like right now—when his actions seemed utterly unconnected to his brain. The unchained tires of his automobile spun, then caught the gravel as he turned onto the driveway of Dani Harmon's farm.

Go figure.

He'd left here half an hour ago, sweating bullets and almost dizzy from the knowledge that he'd inadvertently applied to become someone's husband—sort of. He'd left swiftly, wanting to spare himself and the woman any further embarrassment. If Gene Harmon, the father, hadn't posted that damned misleading help wanted notice, Sam never would have gone near the man's daughter.

It was a hell of a mess, but he'd made a clean escape.

So why was he returning to the scene of the crime?

Sam sighed resignedly. Because escapes were never clean, that's why. Escapes, by their very nature, left threads hanging and moments unfinished, and Sam figured he ought to know. He had enough hanging threads in his life to furnish a quilting bee.

Besides, there had been something in Dani Harmon's smile when they first started talking, something in the way she lowered her gaze, fussed at her tight curls. Here was a woman who could be hurt, and Sam didn't want that possibility hanging over his head.

So he was back to make sure she understood that his aversion to marriage had nothing to do with her personally.

Sam's hands tightened on the steering wheel as the car rocked along the snow and gravel. On the other hand, he considered, perhaps a woman who advertised for a husband didn't take anything personally.

Advertising for a mate. Sam shook his head. Whew! He hardly understood his own era. Yeah, he knew all about loneliness, but to embark on blind date after blind date with no more justification than a few lines of ad copy? And to turn marriage into some kind of a business arrangement?

A wry, self-mocking smile quirked his lips. All in all, not a woman in dire need of having her feelings protected.

Turn the car around, chump. Go back where you came from, or to wherever you think you want to end up, but leave the woman alone. Hell, she's probably forgotten your name by now.

The driveway was wide enough to make a U-turn, so he edged the car to the right in order to begin his turn. He became aware of the woman in the bulky green jacket several yards before she became aware of him. He had ample opportunity to note that Dani Harmon walked with her head down, shoes stomping the snow and gravel like so many bugs she needed to kill. He had ample opportunity to see that she was crying.

It was twenty degrees out, but Sam started sweating like it was summer in Phoenix, Arizona. He cut the engine, took a breath and got out of the car.

Dani realized there was someone else on the road when she heard a door slam. She looked up, blinked through a haze of tears and felt her heart jump into her throat. Mclean!

Quickly, she wiped her face, sniffled and straightened her spine. He was standing next to his car, watching her, a distinctly unfriendly frown on his lean face. She halted the moment she realized he was there, and now she and Mclean appeared to be at a standoff, neither moving, neither saying a word.

He started toward her.

On her way out of the house, she'd donned her father's old green ski jacket, her rattiest mittens and the misshapen wool cap that represented her first attempt to knit. Beneath the cap her curly hair burst like a forest fire.

Bad enough he knew she'd advertised for a husband. It was plain humiliating to appear before him looking like Little Orphan Annie after an Army surplus sale.

Resisting the urge to rip the knit cap from her head, she forced herself to remain absolutely still as he approached. When she could see the whites of his eyes, she fired the biggest, blandest smile she possessed. Her legal receptionist's smile—poised, in control, utterly neutral and impersonal.

Sam stopped walking.

If he'd known what he was going to say before he got out of the car, he forgot. Dani Harmon looked like a deer trapped in the glare of oncoming headlights. He'd seen more genuine smiles on the faces of his troops after a ten-mile march. He wanted to ask if she was all right, but forced himself to curb the impulse. *Get on with it.*

She spoke before he did.

"Mr. Mclean?" She sounded only mildly surprised, as if she hadn't expected to see him again and hadn't particularly cared. "Did you forget something?"

Just my common sense. "No."

She hitched a thumb over her shoulder. "Because if you did, my father is up at the house. I'm just on my way to check the fence."

Bouncing on the balls of her feet as if she couldn't wait to get moving again and was mightily inconvenienced by the delay, Dani raised her eyebrows when he made no attempt to leave. *What?* her expression demanded.

"I didn't forget anything. I came back..." He halted, searching for the right words to apologize for hurting the feelings of a woman who at that moment could have frozen water with her smile. "Look. I didn't feel right leaving the way I..." He scowled. *Hell.* "I want to talk to you about what happened earlier."

Dani cocked her head like a puppy trying to fathom the word *sit.* Apparently neither his coming nor his going had made much of an impression on her. *Oh, did you leave?* her look seemed to say.

Allowing her brow to unfurl slowly—an *Ah, yes, it's coming back to me now* expression—she nodded, then flapped a hand and shook her head. "That," she said, dismissing it easily. "Pop told me about the mix-up. Wasn't that a hoot?" She tossed out a short laugh. "I tell ya."

A hoot?

Sam felt his brow lower notch by notch.

"I'm sorry you came out all this way," she said.

"Which time?"

"Hmm?"

"Which time?" Resting his hands on his hips, Sam narrowed his eyes. "The first time we were both operating under a misconception. Nobody's fault. But this time—" he leaned forward "—this time, Ms. Harmon, I believe I'm getting the brush-off."

"Brush-off?" She appeared sincerely astounded. "I'm not brushing you off, Mr. Mclean. We both realize it was a misunderstanding. I didn't think we had anything more to talk about."

He stared at her for several seconds. "We do."

Crossing her arms, Dani waited reluctantly for him to continue.

He cleared his throat. "I came back," he said, "to apologize for leaving abruptly." He nodded uncomfortably, stirring the air with his hand. "So. I apologize."

The moment the words *I apologize* left his mouth, Sam looked ten pounds lighter. His relief was palpable, as if now that the repentance portion of his afternoon was over, he could get on with his life and try to forget this awkwardness had occurred.

That's how it appeared to Dani, at any rate, and she didn't like it, not one little bit. She felt like she'd gotten a bee sting on top of a mosquito bite and was expected to thank the bee! Put a check mark next to *Apologize to D.H.* and cross her off your to-do list.

"Is that it?" she asked.

Sam frowned. "That's what I came to say."

"Uh-huh. Well, no harm done." Her response was tight and crisp. "Other than a little wasted time. And some disappointment on your part, I imagine, but I'm sure—"

"On *my* part?"

"Being out of work." She shrugged. "Obviously, you needed a job badly. Sorry I had to disappoint you."

Sam worked his jaw so that his lips pursed briefly. "I wasn't too disappointed. My plans are pretty loose." He stood straight, mirroring her body language, with arms crossed over his chest. "I'm sorry *you* were disappointed, though. Obviously you needed a husband—" he rephrased the gibe she'd aimed at him "—badly." He arched a brow. "Et cetera."

Dani's smile spit saccharin. "If you're implying that *you* disappointed *me*, Mr. Mclean, please don't be concerned. I am not disappointed, I am relieved. I placed that ridiculous ad on a whim.''

''A whim.''

''That's right.'' Ignoring the dictionary definition of *whim* as something sudden or capricious—and not, on the other hand, a decision debated ceaselessly for days—Dani fibbed with uncharacteristic abandon. ''I was afraid no one would respond to an ad for a hired hand. I can't pay anything, you see, and obviously I was feeling a little desperate.'' She rolled her eyes. ''Really dumb. I've been working too hard. Fortunately I've come to my senses.''

''Have you? How so?''

''You were my first interview, Mr. Mclean. And my last.''

''Hmm.'' He mulled that over awhile. Shrugging, he tipped his head toward his car. ''May I offer you a ride to your house?''

''Thank you, but no.'' Remembering her original fib, she waved vaguely toward the road. ''I still have to...check on the fence.''

''I can wait.''

''It's not necessary.''

''I thought we could talk more comfortably indoors. You look cold.''

''Talk? But—''

Reaching toward her with his index finger, he almost, but not quite, touched the tip of her nose. ''You're turning pink.''

No longer brooding at all, his attitude now was solicitous, even gentle. Dani frowned warily.

The courtliness she'd found so intriguing earlier once more threatened to draw her into that no-man's-land where she hovered between the impulse to move away and the desire to remain right where she was.

"What do we have to talk about?"

"Employment," Sam said, his hazel gaze focused and intent. "I'd like to reapply for the job."

Chapter Six

Dani waited for the pounding in her ears to subside.

"I can't pay anything," she reminded the man in front of her.

"The notice your father posted said room and board. That's all I expect."

They stood in silence for several moments.

"Why?" Dani asked finally. "You have a nice car." She nodded to the late-model Buick sedan, then gestured to Sam. "Nice clothes. Why would you want to work on a run-down farm in the middle of nowhere for no pay?"

The tiniest of smiles curved his lips. "Does make you wonder, doesn't it?"

"Yes."

He glanced toward the house. "Would you believe it's because of my sweet tooth?"

Dani shook her head, but her lips lifted slightly. She could almost believe it, recalling his first reaction upon entering her home, the way he'd stopped and savored the aroma of her baking. But no man—certainly not this one—would take a job just so he could stock up on chocolate turnovers.

She waited patiently while Sam weighed his words, considering his answer before he spoke.

"I'm not going to be much of a prize, either." There was faint humor in his tone, but his expression was serious, his gaze direct and watchful. "I've never worked on a farm before, run-down or otherwise. I have an injury to my hip that's still pretty new. I'm not sure what my limits will be. As things stand now, sometimes the hip gets the better of me and my leg stiffens." His voice grew taut and gruff as he explained the situation, and she knew the admission was hard for him. "I'm not certain I can give you the full day's work you could get from someone else. But I'll damn well try."

"I didn't notice anything. I mean—"

"I limp," he stated. "I've been compensating, trying to minimize it since I got here, and it's paying me back in spades right now."

No wonder he wanted to go to the house. "I'm sorry, I didn't realize—"

He brushed the apology away. "I didn't want you to. But you asked me why I want to work here, and this—" he tapped his left thigh "—is part of it."

"You can't be in the Army anymore?"

"There's a desk job waiting for me in Florida. I'm considering it."

"Florida. Is that where you're from?"

"No. I've never been there before."

Dani mulled that over. He was considering a job

where he knew no one at all. "You said your injury was part of the reason. Is there another part?" She asked the question tentatively, feeling as if she was prying, admitting to herself that wanting to know had little to do with being a responsible employer. Sam Mclean exuded masculinity, strength and power. And he seemed, of all things, *nice.*

"Are you going to take the desk job?" she asked before he answered the first question.

"I may." He nodded. "Probably."

So his stay here would be temporary. "When does it start?"

"First week of the new year."

"That's only about six weeks away." That would do her little good. "And the holidays are coming up, so really you'd only be here—"

"I'd stay through the holidays. If that's all right with you."

She started to protest—for his sake—then realized he'd just answered her other question. If he had someplace to go, he would. This man who'd played Santa, who had spoken so gently to her little boy, needed a home for the holidays.

Because she *was* a responsible person, she would ask for references and check them tonight. She would verify that there really was a desk job waiting for him somewhere in Florida.

A mild gust of wind made the chimes on her porch ding together. Dusky smoke rose from her chimney—Pop had started a fire. Dani saw Sam's chest expand as he inhaled the aroma of burning oak.

She remembered the early days when she'd first arrived in Idaho. The scent of oak wafting from the chimney had made her feel good, too. Safe and warm. Home.

"Tomorrow," she said, coming to a decision quickly, amazed and a bit frightened by how right the words felt. "You can start tomorrow."

"Will you come away from there!"

Dani's frantic voice carried easily from dining to living room.

Beth Stanley and Carrie Riggs stood on either side of her living room window, peering around the curtains. Dani had drawn her drapes ten minutes ago because the two women had shown a frustrating inability to concentrate with Sam in full view beyond the glass, fixing the porch steps.

"Good bod," Beth, seven months pregnant with her fourth child, murmured, nodding her head.

"He has a face like a Roman chariot racer." Carrie, who at thirty-eight had the dubious honor of being the oldest living never-married woman in Rockview, actually sighed.

"He looks like that actor—" Beth snapped her fingers "—what's-his-face, Indiana Jones."

"Harrison Ford." Carrie nodded.

"Great shoulders."

"Noble forehead."

"Nice a—"

"*Stop it!*" Dani rushed to the window. "Both of you! Stop it right this minute. This is embarrassing." Grabbing Carrie's skinny arm and Beth's pudgy one, she dragged the women into the dining room. "Please! Sit down now. We're supposed to be working." She crossed around the table, reminding her friends sternly, "The holiday bazaar is only two weeks away. We haven't even reviewed the raffle donations yet."

"Dani's right." Plopping herself into a chair, Beth reached for one of the notepads and pens Dani had laid out earlier. "Let's concentrate on church." A Cheshire-cat grin pressed deep dimples into her cheeks. "I'm just full of ideas today for creative original sin."

Carrie twittered, happily scandalized, but Dani put her foot down. "Do you need something to settle yourselves? Hot tea?" She glared at Beth. "Valium?"

Modulating her grin to a mischievous smile, Beth shrugged. "Don't be a killjoy, sweetie. We have to have *some* fun."

Dani jerked a chair away from the table. She was torn between guilt over snapping at her friends and irritation at the way they were responding to the news she'd hired Sam. "Well, why don't you drool over Arnie?" she grumbled.

"Drool over my husband?" Beth looked at Dani as if she'd lost her marbles. "Sweetie, I'm seven months pregnant. I pee twelve times a day, sleep five minutes a night and have only the vaguest memory of my breasts ever pointing north. On top of that, I am not eagerly awaiting the miracle of my fourth labor. If Lamaze is ever going to work, they'd better start teaching women how to pant 'epidural' during contractions." She shook her head sadly. "And you want me to drool over my husband."

Carrie waited for her to finish, then leaned toward

Dani and petitioned eagerly. "Tell us again how you found him."

"I didn't find him." Dani pushed a red curl behind her ear and shrugged. "I told you, he answered an ad."

"An ad you never even mentioned you were going to place," Beth admonished.

"My father wrote it. I'm not even sure what it said."

Beth and Carrie had been her friends since the first week she'd moved to Idaho. They were loving, supportive and loyal to the nth degree, but she could not bring herself to tell them of her original intention to find a husband. She just couldn't. It had turned out to be too humiliating.

Briefly she explained that Sam had been working at Lawson's, had seen the notice her father posted on the store's community bulletin board and had called for an interview. End of story.

"He was playing Santa?" Beth pressed a hand to her heart. "That's so *cute*."

Carrie turned wide round eyes to Dani. "When did he start working for you?"

"Yesterday. And I checked his references first."

"Good for you," Beth commended. "Who were they?"

"The owner of Lawson's, who's a friend of his, I guess, and the post commander of his Army base."

"His Army base?" Beth drew back, sitting up as straight as pregnancy allowed. "Officer or enlisted man?"

"Officer. He's a sergeant first class."

"Oh, *yes!*" She thrust both hands in the air,

thumbs up, like a rabid Siskel and Ebert. "This is just like that movie—" she waved a hand "—what was it? Where Debra Winger works in a factory and Richard Gere—"

"*An Officer and a Gentleman!*" Carrie supplied enthusiastically. "Only Richard Gere wasn't in the Army, he was in the Naval Aviation Corps. It was so romantic." She leaned over the table and whispered confidentially, "They had a lot of S-E-X in that movie."

Beth nodded. "Uh-huh. So tell us about Mr. Fix-It. Is the boy single or what?"

Dani frowned. "I don't know. I think so."

"You *think?* You didn't ask?" Shaking her head in disgust, Beth admonished, "Oh, girls, girls! You see, this is why I get upset. Look, I know I complain about marriage, but only when I'm this pregnant. Marriage is really great. I recommend it. But the two of you—" she waved her hand to include Carrie, too "—have got to get real. This isn't exactly the Hard Rock Café. Need I remind you that pickin's are slim around here?" She honed in on Dani. "You have beyond that front door a tall, handsome Army officer who played *Santa,* for glory's sake! Can you honestly tell me you aren't interested?"

"I am not interested."

Beth wagged a finger. "I said honestly. Where's he staying?"

"In the attic bedroom."

"The attic bedroom. *Your* attic bedroom?" She grew more eager by the moment. "What did you make for dinner last night?"

Dani rolled her eyes. "Pot roast and potato pancakes." She gestured to the papers on her dining table. "Now could we please get back to—"

Beth crowed with delight, rubbing her hands. "Home cooking." She glanced at Carrie. "She likes this guy. So," she said, returning a razor-sharp gaze to Dani, "tell us about dinner. Was he appreciative?"

Carrie quivered with interest. "Is he a good eater?"

"Did he talk much?"

"Are his manners graceful?"

Dani groaned. She didn't want to think about dinner. She'd hardly slept a wink all night because no matter how much she'd tried, she hadn't been able to *stop* thinking about it.

Carrie scooted toward her, her eyes sparkling and earnest. "Oh, please tell us, Dani. I know it's perfectly awful that we're going on like this, but I have no other way of learning about these things."

Dani looked at her friend and felt her resistance soften. All right, so it hadn't been a common night, no matter how she tried to tell herself otherwise. Having Sam Mclean at her table and in her home had turned mundane into...

The word that popped into mind made her cringe with self-consciousness.

Having Sam Mclean to dinner had turned mundane into dreamy.

Yes, he ate heartily and was more than appreciative.

No, he didn't talk much, but he had excellent manners and his voice thrilled her so much that *please pass the peas* gave her goose bumps.

Last evening he'd addressed her father deferentially, her son with patience and care. He'd smiled when he tasted something he especially liked and thanked her over the top of the glassware with his eyes as well as his words.

And then...

Dani closed her eyes, reliving the moment, seeing all the tiny details, willing the image to last.

"He washed the dishes," she said, her words hushed.

"He washed the dishes?" For once, even Beth's exuberance was muted with awe. "Really?"

Dani nodded.

"Did you have to ask?"

She shook her head. It wasn't *what* Sam had done that affected her so strongly, but rather *how* he had done it, and why.

Rising from the table, she had reached for Timmy's plate, her back and shoulders still aching from the baking and packaging she'd completed early that morning. Pop had made most of the deliveries for her, covering a radius of almost one hundred miles, and the kitchen was relatively clear. She'd set out an apple-raisin pie for their dessert.

As her hand went to Timmy's milk glass, Sam stopped her.

"I'll get that." He pushed back his chair.

"I want to clear the table," Dani said, thinking he intended to get Timmy more milk. "I thought we'd have dessert a little later. Pop likes to have his in the living room."

Sam smiled. "Why don't you relax with your father," he told his new employer. "We'll get the dishes."

"We?"

"Tim and I."

Both Dani and her father froze mid-motion. Half-way out of his chair, Gene looked at the stranger with new interest and nodded in approval. "Guess I should have thought of that myself awhile ago." He rose, carried his plate and glass to the sink and said, "I'll see you in the living room, daughter. Last one to the remote control is a rotten egg."

Dani stayed where she was, not sure how to address such an offer when it came from a man she still considered a guest in her home.

"That's very nice of you," she began haltingly, "but it isn't necessary. You're not here to do the domestic chores."

"Uh-oh." Compressing his lips, Sam wagged his head. "Ms. Harmon, I hope you're not going to turn out to be one of those downright sexist employers." He cocked a brow, humor peeking from the depths of his hazel eyes.

Dani was caught off guard. She opened her mouth to protest, then recognized his playfulness and found herself grinning in return. "If I do, you can report me to the labor board, Mr. Mclean."

"Mommy, what's a labor board?" Timmy watched their exchange, the heels of his tennis shoes thumping rhythmically against the legs of his chair.

"It's... I'll explain it later." To Sam, she said, "Why don't *you* go watch TV? You worked really hard today. Seriously."

"Seriously, so did you." He turned to Timmy.

"What do you say, Tim? Your mother's had a long day and made us a fine meal. Think we ought to do the dishes?"

"Just us two?" Timmy looked surprised and pleased by the prospect.

Sam narrowed his eyes as if considering their ability to do the job. After a moment, he nodded. "We're man enough."

Giving Sam the sweet, pearly toothed smile that never failed to melt his mother's heart, Timmy nodded enthusiastically. His amber curls flip-flopped.

Dani hovered, finding inconsequential tasks to occupy herself in the kitchen while Sam set her son up on a chair by the sink. He gave the five-year-old the task of holding the cups and plates under the faucet for a quick rinse after Sam soaped them. Dani bit her tongue, refraining from warning against splashing, but Sam was a step ahead of her.

"Wait a minute, troop," he said, tucking a dish towel into the waistband of Timmy's jeans.

When Timmy wanted to know what a troop was, Sam gave him a thumbnail description of Army life, adjusted for young ears. The conversation was still going strong when Dani finally left the kitchen.

"What happened after that?"

"Hmm?"

"What happened after he did the dishes?" Beth prodded.

"Nothing," she told her friends. "He was very sweet...to Timmy...and then—" she shrugged "—he went upstairs."

"I wonder how long it's been since he had sex."

"Beth, for heaven's sake!" Dani's gaze flew to

the door. Carrie's chin slid off her palm and nearly hit the table.

"What?" Beth shrugged. "He can't hear me, and we're all women here. We do think about these things, right? Don't tell me you haven't wondered." She pinned Dani with a don't-fib gaze.

"I don't wonder," Dani insisted, arranging pencils in a neat row. "He's a man. It can't be that long."

"Chauvinist." Beth grinned. She splayed her hands on the table. "All right, what are we going to do about this?"

"Well, I thought if Carrie handles cash at the door, then you and I could—" Dani began.

"I'm not talking about the holiday bazaar."

"I know exactly what you're talking about," Dani acknowledged, pushing her fingers through her hair. "I am deliberately changing the subject to avoid arguing with you. No one is doing anything about Sam Mclean, at least not as far as I'm concerned." Her gaze flicked to Carrie. "If you're interested, be my guest. Pursue him all you want, with my blessing."

Carrie gasped, putting her fingers with their neatly trimmed, utilitarian fingernails to her lips. "Me? Heavens, I couldn't, I would never... A man like that?" She shivered. "He looks so...imposing."

Dani shrugged. "Fine. That's that, then."

Brusquely, she got down to business, praying there would be no more talk about her employee. Beth and Carrie exchanged a look that Dani chose to ignore, but they zipped their lips—Beth exerting visible effort to do so—for the rest of the afternoon, and the three women managed to iron out the final details of the holiday bazaar.

Dani never stopped thinking about Sam.

Even for a minute.

She'd discovered at breakfast this morning that Sam's consideration the evening before had not been an anomaly. After thanking her for another fine meal, he carried his dish and coffee cup to the sink. When Timmy followed suit, carefully setting his plate and milk glass on the counter, Sam winked at the boy like they had a secret. Timmy's chest puffed out as proud as a rooster's, and Dani—Lord help her— thought, *Well, this is how it was meant to be.*

Around one o'clock, as Beth and Carrie argued over whether tins of peanut brittle could be considered a craft—only if the tins were hand-painted, they decided—Sam popped into the house to tell Dani he was going into town for supplies and to ask directions to the hardware store.

Hoping he was somehow oblivious to the way Beth and Carrie stared at him, Dani asked if he wanted lunch before he left, but Sam declined, noting that he could see she was busy and would be happy to pick up something in town.

Beth's eyebrows rose higher than should have been humanly possible. *What a catch,* she communicated to Dani. Carrie merely gazed and twittered.

It was a relief to see Sam go, and an even bigger relief to conclude the meeting an hour later.

Beth and Carrie left a few minutes before Gene walked through the door with Timmy.

"Look what I found at the kindergarten."

"Thanks for picking my munchkin up, Pop. It was Jeanne Reynold's turn for the carpool, but she came down with the flu." Scooping Timmy off his feet and swinging him around the living room, Dani asked happily, "How was school, you whirling dervish?"

Timmy giggled and squealed. "What's that?" he asked as she collapsed with him in a breathless heap on the couch.

"What's what, Mr. Monkey?"

"A worrying—" he frowned "—dirsh."

"Dervish." Dani sat back as Timmy draped himself across her lap. "Mmm, it's like the Tasmanian Devil on *The Roadrunner* cartoon."

"He goes fast!"

"Uh-huh." She pulled Timmy's cap off his head and ran slender fingers through the red curls. "You need a haircut."

"Yuh." Gene nodded, hanging his coat and hat on the rack inside the door. "I told him that."

Ignoring a discussion of something he wanted no part of, Timmy slid off his mother's lap. "Where's Sam?"

"He went to the hardware store."

Timmy jumped up and down. In a tone suspiciously like a whine, he declared, "I wanna go!"

"He already left, I said." Dani unbuttoned his coat. "Besides, Sam is working for us, honey. We have to let him do his job without bothering him."

In an effort to forestall the protest she saw coming, Dani asked, "Where's your knapsack?"

"It's not a knapsack, it's a backpack."

"Oh. Sorry."

"I've got it." Gene lifted it by a strap, and Dani smiled gratefully. Without prompting, Timmy remembered to bring the nylon sack home once a week, max.

"Did you thank Granpop for picking you up today, pup?"

"Thank you." He ran to get the backpack. "We did finger painting, and Mrs. Karp let us put rice on them. I'm gonna show Sam when he gets back!" Energized by the thought, he ran to his room.

It was the first time Timmy missed an opportunity to share his artwork with his grandfather.

"Sorry, Pop." Dani clasped her hands together on her knees and sat forward. "He's just so excited about having someone new in the house."

Gene nodded. "So what are you sorry for?"

"Well, I—" Dani shrugged "—I don't want you to feel…"

Gene smiled when she stumbled. "Timmy knows who his grandpa is. Nothing's gonna get in the way of that."

"Maybe it's not good for him to be so informal with Sam. I thought it was okay, but maybe—"

"It is good. They get along real well."

"Mclean's a stranger to us."

Gene shook his head the way he did when he'd already given something considerable thought. "A stranger's someone who doesn't belong. Sam fits in fine. Looks more comfortable on a farm than we did when we first got here." A twinkle lit the older man's eyes. "Looks like he's real comfortable in your kitchen, too."

"He does like his food," Dani agreed with a smile. She plucked at the piping on the sofa cushion.

"He's leaving soon, you know. Probably right after Christmas."

"Probably." Gene started toward the kitchen, a hand on his softly rounded belly. "Got any more of those brownies with the marshmallows?"

"The rocky road bars? They're in the freezer."

"I like 'em frozen."

Smiling, Dani rose from the couch. She slung an arm around her father's shoulders as they walked to the kitchen. "Your cholesterol feeling a little low today, is it?"

"Never mind." He gave her a squeeze. "I like this time of year, I really do. Everyone's the same age at Christmas, you ever notice that?"

Dani grinned as she opened the freezer. "I'm beginning to."

"I like that my birthday falls during this time of year, too."

"Is that a hint?"

"Nope. Just yakking." Gene poured himself a cup of the coffee left from Dani's meeting. "Want a cup?" When she shook her head, he seated himself at the table. "Makes sense to have a birthday this time of year, Christmas being the season of birth and all. Beginnings. Makes me feel like I get a chance to start from scratch every year, see what I can muck up this time."

He spoke with infectious humor, and Dani smiled at him. "No one ever really starts from scratch, though," she said.

"No. And most wouldn't want to. Still, the idea of beginning all over again is appealing sometimes, isn't it?" He bit into a brownie, rich and fudgy despite the freezer, and shook his head. "I have to tell you, that is good."

"Think so? I'm going to push them around Valentine's Day."

Her father grinned. "Shouldn't have to push too hard."

"No, not if I sell them all to you!"

With her elbow on the table and her chin on her palm, Dani pondered her father's comment about starting over. "Why is it so appealing to start over? You'd forget all your mistakes. Then you'd make them all over again."

"Yup. On the other hand, you wouldn't be afraid of them anymore."

Gene ate and Dani thought some more. She'd been so fortunate to have her father to guide and support her these past few years. He'd been living in an apartment in Long Beach, California, selling gold jewelry door-to-door, when she'd asked him to move in with her and Timmy in Idaho. Gene had liked his life in California, but he hadn't even hesitated.

Merely sitting with him now made Dani feel calm—until he started talking about new beginnings and old mistakes. Dani tapped fingers against the table. What good was a mistake if you didn't learn from it? Take her mistakes with men, for instance. She'd learned well not to romanticize the male-female relationship. She'd been running scared lately, behaving foolishly, and for no good reason. Her little family of three was doing fine, just fine.

"So you think Sam'll be gone by New Year's, hmm?"

The question jarred her from her thoughts. She sat up straight. "I think so."

"Well, that's not *too* soon," Gene said, refuting her earlier comment.

"Sure it is. Christmas is only three weeks away."

Gene shook his head. "Daughter, where you and Sam are concerned, something tells me you've got a long way to go yet before Christmas."

Chapter Seven

In the battle to remain a spectator rather than a participant in Dani Harmon's family, Sam lost a little more ground every day.

He'd been here a week now, seven days of sitting at a table where a child's laughter serenaded each meal, seven nights of accepting fresh towels that smelled like rain and powder from a woman who smelled like sunshine and flowers.

A whole glorious, torturous week of chomping at the bit to finish his work each day so he could rejoin this family each night.

He'd never felt less alone in his life.

There were times, in fact, when he felt so good, it scared him.

So far, he'd avoided being alone with Dani except at lunch, when Gene was off making deliveries for her or conducting his door-to-door sales, and Timmy was at school. Then Sam would indulge himself, warming his hands around a mug of the fragrant coffee she brewed just before he came in, warming his soul by sitting very still, watching her as she moved with characteristic grace and purpose.

They spoke, of course, but never about anything personal. Sam thought that was his choice until he realized she never attempted to deepen the conversation, either. They stuck to two topics of interest to both of them—the farm and Timmy.

And yet, though the conversation was not intimate, the distance between them was closing. He could feel it happening.

He could feel it right now.

Against the wall that divided living from dining room, Dani had an old spinet piano. The instrument was piled with sheet music and songbooks. Tonight was the first time she'd played in Sam's presence, and the evening's musical selection was a series of Christmas songs that were going to be performed in the holiday pageant at Timmy's school. At the moment, Dani was helping her son learn a song about pinecones, holly berries and popcorn balls. Gene relaxed on the couch, nodding in time to the music.

Outside, the temperature dipped below freezing, but inside logs glowed and crackled in the brick hearth, and the soft lighting Dani seemed to prefer cast a rich, buttery glow on the room and its inhabitants.

In the easy chair that had become more or less his since he'd moved in, Sam pretended to read the newspaper. In fact, he couldn't have cared less at the moment about what Congress was or wasn't doing. The only current event worth noting were Dani's hands, slender and curved, as they flowed across the keys.

She sang along with her son, and her voice was surprisingly husky.

"Big breath now," she coached as she led them into the final reprise.

When the song ended, Dani clapped her hands, then pulled Timmy closer to her on the piano bench, wrapping an arm around his small shoulders. Her hand lingered on his thin back, rubbing in a gentle, circling motion, an unconscious expression of the love that filled every exchange between her and her son.

"Hey, that was good." Gene stood and walked to the piano. "Play 'White Christmas,'" he instructed, taking his place by the piano and preparing to sing. "Come over here, Sam." He gestured while Dani played the introduction. "You know this one, don't you?"

Tension swelled in Sam's chest. He held up one hand, gripping his newspaper in the other. "No, thanks, I'll be the audience."

Shrugging, Gene began an enthusiastic rendition of the old Bing Crosby song. Accompanying her father on the piano, Dani was turned away from Sam, and he was glad. As he breathed with the music, his tension slowly faded.

The impulse to get up, go over to that piano and sing amid their little family was stronger than they could possibly know, but when the words to the song rose to his lips, he sang silently, staying put in the chair.

It had been nearly a dozen years since Sam had

belonged to a family. He had grown up mostly on his own. His mother had worked two jobs to keep a meager amount of money coming in to the household, then spent the majority of her free time "unwinding" in a local bar with her boyfriend. As for his father, Sam had never met the man and probably never would. It no longer bothered him. Some men were not cut out to be fathers.

At nineteen, after a few aimless years working at nowhere jobs, Sam had joined the Army and found a life. He'd worked hard, developed a discipline that was unshakable and became an officer training candidate. Then he found a personal life in the home of his post commander.

The colonel and his wife invited Sam home one Thanksgiving. That holiday marked the first time Sam sat at a table covered with a linen cloth and candlesticks, china and decorations and with people who lingered after the meal was done, talking about something more than who'd gotten sacked the week before or who was going to win the Rusty Tavern's next big pool tournament. The night was engraved indelibly on his memory.

When they asked him for Christmas, Sam went.

And met the colonel's daughter, who was home from college.

And ruined everything with one stupid act that changed all their lives.

Candace had been beautiful, headstrong and eager to flout her father's strict authority by engaging in a tryst with one of his men. Sam had been young, foolish and greedy. The colonel and his wife had given him a chance to taste a new and better life, and he'd repaid them by having a one-night fling with their daughter. That mistake had been merely the first in a series.

Gene and Dani ended their song with a flourish, applauding each other and laughing when Gene reached for a high note. Dani tried to persuade her father to sing another tune, but he shook his head, patted his daughter's shoulder and the top of the spinet in thanks, then returned to his place on the couch.

Dani swiveled on the piano bench. "Any other requests?"

She looked straight at Sam.

Song titles came to mind like a dozen wild ideas, freely and eagerly. It took an effort not to speak them, but in the past ten years Sam had honed his ability to restrain himself, the way an athlete restrains his appetite. *No.* He shook his head. *No requests.*

Dani smiled and turned to her son. "How about running through the rest of the songs you'll be singing at the pageant, pup?"

Watching his feet as they swung back and forth beneath the bench, Timmy shook his head.

"No?" Puzzled, Dani pushed a russet curl off his forehead. "Why not?"

Timmy shrugged.

The atmosphere in the living room changed abruptly. Sullenness was so uncharacteristic of the little boy, even Sam found it impossible to dismiss his sudden moodiness. Tim had been chattering about the holiday show for days.

"We haven't practiced 'Rudolph the Red-Nosed

Reindeer' yet.'' Dani reached for a new sheet of music. ''You love that one.''

''No, I don't.'' The words were mumbled, but obstinate. ''It's stupid!''

Dani placed both hands in her lap and focused all her attention on her son. ''Honey, what's wrong? I thought you were very excited about the pageant.''

Timmy jumped off the piano bench. ''I am not excited! I don't want to sing in a dumb old pageant. It's stupid and dumb!''

''Hey, hey...'' Reaching for Timmy's arm before he could run out of the room, Dani held him still and murmured soothingly, coaxing him to calm down and focus on her. ''Now tell me why you don't want to be in the show.''

''Do I *have* to be in it?''

Dani struggled not to sigh. ''I don't know yet. First tell me why you don't want to.''

Timmy looked at his mother with huge, soulful eyes. ''Everybody gets to have people they want to come.''

''Well, honey, so do you.''

''Nuh-uh. Alex gets to have his baby sister, and she's too little even to know the songs. And Grady got to ask his cousins.'' Timmy looked at his sneakers. A sad, trembling pout pushed his bottom lip out. He mumbled something Dani couldn't understand.

''What?''

Raising his head, Timmy blurted, ''I told 'em I was gonna bring Sam and they said I couldn't 'cause he isn't family!''

Dani looked at her son in dismay. Of course, he could bring Sam. Timmy's class was small. Each child could have unlimited guests. The kids who told him otherwise were just being...kids.

But, of course, that didn't address the issue of whether Sam wanted to go.

She glanced at the man in question from the corner of her eye, trying to gauge his response to this development. His face could close so suddenly sometimes, hiding expression like the sun behind a cloud. Right now he was looking at Timmy with features that were set and firm, but unreadable.

Do not hurt my child, she warned silently, her mind whirring like a top as she tried to think of ways to let her son down gently. What if he was viewing Sam as a father figure already? She may have made her worst mistake yet by allowing this man into her home and their lives.

When Sam stood, Dani tensed. He started toward them, and in a fiercely protective move, she reached for her son, drawing him in close. Sam's eyes widened as he acknowledged the gesture, but he kept coming. Dani's heart filled her throat as he knelt before them.

"Tim." Eye level with the solemn little boy, he spoke man-to-man. "I don't know much about Christmas pageants and things like that. But I bet your teacher wouldn't mind if you asked someone outside your family."

Briefly, he glanced to Dani for confirmation, and she nodded, but she got the impression it didn't matter what Timmy's teacher said. Sam had made up his mind to go.

"Okay." Returning his gaze to Timmy, he smiled.

"As long as I can get the time off from work, I'd be glad to attend. We'll have to check with the boss."

"Who's the boss?"

"Your mom."

"Oh, yeah." Timmy's big green eyes flashed surprise and then pleasure. "Oh, boy!" He put his hands on the piano bench and bounced up and down on his toes. "Can he, Mommy? Can he, can he?"

Dani grinned at the rapid return of her son's joie de vivre. "Yes." She nodded. "Sam can come with us."

"Yeah!" Timmy turned and hopped around the room with both legs together, like a Pogo stick.

Glancing almost shyly at the man whose presence had caused all the commotion, Dani said quietly, "That was very nice of you."

Sam looked at her a long moment. Standing, shoving his hands in his pockets, he asked, "Does he get picked on often?"

The low mumble was intended for Dani's ears only. Timmy was too busy bouncing and chattering to overhear.

Dani stared at Sam in growing wonder. He looked ready to take on an army for her child's sake.

"He wasn't being picked on," she said softly. "Not really. Kids do that to each other all the time. It's a kind of juvenile one-upmanship. They're cutting their adult teeth on each other."

Sam appeared doubtful for a moment, then nodded. "He seems okay now."

"He is." *Well, darn you, Sam Mclean.* If Beth found out about this, she'd have a shotgun and a minister over here by morning.

Was ever a man so full of surprises?

Over on the sofa, Pop shook his head while he watched his grandson's antics. Finally, he rose and announced, "That's it for me. I'm going to bed." He shot Timmy a no-nonsense look. "I think it's time for you to turn in, too."

Timmy started to protest, but quieted immediately when his mother seconded the motion. "Good idea."

Timmy wasn't about to rock the boat, so instead of fussing, he ran to Sam, standing toe-to-toe with the big man. He craned his neck to look up. "Do you have onions?"

"What?" Sam looked down, bemused.

"Do you have onions? I like to walk on Granpop's feet, only he says I'm getting too big for his onions."

"His—oh." Sam glanced at Gene, and the two men shared a smile. *Bunions*. "No, I don't have any onions, Tim. Not yet."

"Can I walk on your feet to my bedroom?"

"Well…"

"Honey," Dani intervened, shaking her head, "I don't think—"

"You'll have to show me how to do it." Sam's words overlapped hers and, as far as Timmy was concerned, canceled them completely.

"I stand on your feet and then you walk."

Enthusiastically, the five-year-old climbed aboard without further invitation. He held onto Sam's waist, clutching his belt buckle and grinning, ready for his free ride. Like a puppy, he engaged Sam in play as if it was the most natural thing in the world.

Looking into the eager upturned face, Sam answered with a smile of his own, curving and lopsided, a smile that seemed to be directed as much at himself as it was at Timmy.

"Okay, hang on."

He took the long way around the living room, circling the couch, pretending to lose balance at one point.

Dani stared after them as they maneuvered past Gene and down the hallway to Timmy's room. Though Sam's limp was still noticeable, it was less pronounced than it had been earlier in the week. If his leg or hip hurt while he was walking Timmy around the house, he didn't show it.

"Nice fella," Gene said from the entrance to the hallway.

Dani nodded.

"See you in the morning, sweetheart."

"It's barely nine o'clock," Dani protested. "Aren't you going to stay up for the news?"

"Naw, not tonight. Got a big day tomorrow, collecting my accounts. 'Night."

"Good night."

Dani closed the piano lid, tidied her sheet music, then wandered around the room, trying to give Sam time to make a clean getaway before she went to tuck her son in for the night. Sam usually retreated to his room about the same time Gene retired for the night.

Dani straightened the coffee table, picked a toy car off the floor, patted the sofa cushions into place, all the while seeing her child's delighted face and recalling his laughter as Sam walked with him around the room.

How wonderful it would be if a woman could somehow possess an adult's sensibilities and a child's freedom. Hurtling oneself into someone's arms and feeling certain of the reception—wouldn't that be a grand thing to try, at least once?

Dani gazed into the fireplace, content to muse for several moments. Finally, convinced by the quiet that everyone was in his own room, she headed down the hallway. She was outside her son's door before she realized he was already halfway through his prayers.

"God bless Pete and Jack Henry and that new kid Billy Somethin' and please fix it so he doesn't barf in the cloakroom anymore, and bless Mrs. Karp and Mrs. Nichols and..." He paused, trying to remember if he'd left anyone out. "Oh, yeah, and thank You for making it so Sam can come to the Christmas pageant, amen."

Scrambling from his position by the side of the bed, Timmy crawled under the covers.

Dani started to enter the room but stopped when Sam walked into her line of vision. Peering around the door frame, she realized he must have been standing across the room near the dresser.

"Good prayers," he told Timmy, standing at the foot of the bed. "Thanks for including me."

Timmy nodded. "I did last night, too. I asked God to fix your leg. Is it sore? Is that why you sometimes walk funny?"

Dani had to stifle a gasp. Another fine example of a child's spontaneity!

Fortunately Sam did not appear offended in the slightest. He merely nodded and answered, "It hurts a little sometimes. Thanks for asking God to fix it."

"You're welcome." Timmy's silky brows puckered in a frown. "I asked Him to fix my guinea pig, Charlie, last summer, but it didn't work."

"What was wrong with Charlie?"

"My mom ran over him in the driveway."

Tucked behind the door where she was sure they couldn't see her, Dani winced. Peeking further into the room, she could see that Sam was torn between a sympathetic frown and a smile.

"I'm sorry to hear that," he said. He stood with both his hands in the pockets of his jeans. The honey-eyed glow from the lamp did glorious things to his hair, dusting the deep chestnut locks with highlights so richly auburn that for a moment Dani thought he and Timmy could almost be—

Careful! she slammed the brakes on that notion before she completed it. *Daydream alert! Don't go there.*

In Timmy's room, conversation continued casually. "I had a rabbit once," Sam said.

"What was his name?"

"Odenfaden."

Timmy giggled. "That's a funny name."

"Yeah."

"What happened to him?"

There was a brief pause. "Same thing that happened to Charlie."

Timmy's eyes widened. Lowering his gaze, he plucked at the bedcovers. "Were you mad?"

"Sure," Sam answered quietly. "I knew it was an accident, but I was still mad for awhile."

"Did God bring your rabbit back?"

Sam thought that one over for a minute. "I forgot to ask Him. You know what, though?"

"What?"

"My leg feels a lot better already."

"Really? Lots?" Timmy sat up.

"Really."

"A little lot or whole lots?"

Sam grinned. "A whole lots. I'll get your mom to tuck you in now."

"Okay." Timmy wriggled beneath the covers, a big, beautiful smile on his face.

Backing away from the door, Dani turned and ran lightly on her toes down the hall. In the living room, she rushed to the couch, grabbed a magazine and started flipping the pages. Even though she expected it, Sam's voice nearly made her jump.

"Timmy's ready for you to tuck him in."

"Oh, fine. Thank you." She put the magazine down and stood. She had no idea why she was pretending not to have overheard. Timmy was, after all, her son. She didn't have to apologize for checking on him. But somehow Sam's conversation with him had seemed personal, and so dear.

Sam stepped aside to let her pass into the hallway.

"Thank you." Tentatively, she smiled at him.

He nodded, then called to her as she continued down the hall. "Dani?"

She turned and saw him raise something in his hand.

"You dropped this." One of her gold-colored hair combs glittered between his fingers.

Dani's hand flew to the back of her head, feeling for the comb. The gleam in Sam's eyes and the slow, liquid arch of his brow said he knew exactly when she had lost it.

Okay. To listen at your five-year-old son's door was perfectly acceptable. To be caught pretending you hadn't been listening was perfectly humiliating.

Mustering what meager dignity she could, Dani walked back to retrieve her comb. When she reached for it, however, Sam surprised her by tightening his hold. They stared at each other a moment, Sam holding her comb, Dani holding his hand. For one brief, breathless glitch in time, she thought he was going to put the comb in place himself. A private, ineluctable silence wrapped around them as the hazel eyes she was coming to know so well narrowed and darkened.

Dani.

Did he whisper the word or was her mind admonishing her? *Dani, don't linger.... Dani, don't leave....*

His forehead, his cheeks, his jaw—every line, every angle seemed to have been sculpted from the smoothest stone. If he tried to kiss her now, this stranger, this mystery man whom she knew only through his actions, well...she would let him.

He didn't, though, and for an instant Dani wished she was someone else. Someone who would let her lips go all pouty, move forward with clear intent and let the man she desired have it right on the smacker. Someone who wouldn't wonder for five hours afterward, *What does he think of me? What if he hated it? What if he liked it? What now?*

Moot point, she realized, as Sam turned his hand, releasing the hair ornament into her trembling fingers.

She lowered her hand, mumbled, ''Thanks,'' and

retreated down the hallway to tuck in her son. A five-year-old male was more her speed.

Sam stood just inside the living room, watching Dani flee down the hall.

What a hell of a week!

He'd arrived here with his hip and leg still a problem, but at least his head had been screwed on straight, or so he'd thought. Now his leg felt much better, but his head was swimming.

He walked into the living room and sat in his chair.

His chair.

Well, that was part of the problem right there. He was thinking in terms of possession. And nothing here belonged to him, not the chair, not the tools he'd bought with Dani's household accounts money, not the pillow he laid his head on each night—and not the little boy who'd just stood on his feet and asked Sam to stay while he recited his prayers.

He prayed for my leg.

It was a blessing from a child, as pure, as holy as if it had been papal.

Having a little trouble keeping your distance, Mclean?

He pressed his thumb and forefinger against his eyelids. Standing, putting some distance between himself and *his* chair, Sam wandered to the piano—where music and the scent of roses lingered.

There was a tube of hand cream, he knew, on the kitchen sink next to the soap dispenser. Dani used it frequently. Like a voyeur, he had watched her smooth the lotion onto her hands, then push up her sleeves and massage it onto arms as pale and graceful as a ballerina's. She left a subtle, tantalizing trail of perfume wherever she went. Like roses in winter.

He was doomed to wondering. He couldn't look at the bright-eyed, gamin face of the little boy and not wonder about the woman who raised him. She was beautiful, at once the most ethereal and most earthy woman he'd ever met. And so, wondering about the mother led inevitably to wondering about the father.

Who was he? *Where* was he?

Sam had looked for photos—on the wall, on the bookshelf, atop Timmy's dresser, all the obvious places. As far as he could tell, there were no pictures of Timmy's father on display. This and the fact that Dani used the last name Harmon—same as Gene— led Sam to wonder if she'd ever been married.

Sam had no particular judgment about women who had children out of wedlock. He knew too well that some men were useless to their mates, married or not. But somehow he found it difficult to believe that a woman like Dani would choose to have a child on her own.

She was a born nurturer and a traditionalist. The way she stopped anything she was doing to run out and meet the car pool each afternoon, the way she laughed when Timmy told the same joke for the umpteenth time, even the way she called them all in to supper, minding for their sakes more than her own that the dinner she'd cooked be eaten while it was still hot—she was a 1950s Donna Reed woman in 1990s jeans.

And then there was that faraway, dream-catching look in her eyes when she gazed out the kitchen window after supper, into a night too dark to reveal anything except her own thoughts. There were evenings when she nearly brought him to his knees with that look.

She ought to be married. She would turn a common man into a king if she were his bride.

A log crackled and shifted in the fireplace, sending bright orange sparks shooting up the chimney. Sam gazed at the hearth and realized he wasn't only staring at a fire, he was playing with one.

This boy and, more to the point, this woman had the power to make him forget.

Even now, when he could be making a clean getaway simply by retiring to his room for the night, when he *ought* to be making a clean getaway...

He had no intention of doing it.

Chapter Eight

Sam was still there when Dani returned to the living room.

He stood gazing into the fire, wearing one of those brooding Heathcliff expressions that made women forget everything they'd ever learned about smart women and foolish choices.

Running down the hall was not an option, so Dani took a deep breath and stepped forward.

"Okay, I admit it," she announced, spreading her arms wide, then letting them fall. "I did watch you and Timmy from the doorway without announcing myself." She moved until she was behind the couch. "I didn't want to spoil the moment. You're very good with him."

Sam had looked over his shoulder at the first sound of her voice. Now he turned toward her completely, firelight dancing in his dark hair and illuminating features that slid from moody to surprised to humbly pleased. Smiling slightly, he shook his head.

"I don't know much about kids." His tone acknowledged a gross understatement.

"Timmy likes you."

"I like him, too."

Dani ran a finger along the piping on the sofa cushion. "I was, um, sorry to hear about your rabbit." A shallow dimple appeared in her cheek. "Odenfaden, was it?"

Closing his eyes briefly, shaking his head, Sam walked toward her until he was standing near the coffee table on the opposite side of the couch. "Yeah. Look—" he scratched the bridge of his nose "—I made some of that up."

Dani cocked her head in question.

Sam's voice crackled with nuance as he admitted, "I did have a rabbit, but her name was Sheila, not Odenfaden, and she wasn't run over by a car."

"She wasn't?"

He shook his head. "Sheila was probably the oldest living rabbit in Douglas County. She ate a spark plug once. Never even belched."

Dani folded her arms. "Okay, I'm stumped. Why did you—"

"Dani, when Tim mentioned his guinea pig, I..." Passing a hand over his face, Sam sighed. His brief smile was part self-mockery, part apology. "I wanted to say something comforting. Hell, I'm not good at this."

Dani looked at him with awe. "You're great."

Her softly spoken words made time stop. Sam opened his mouth as if to refute her statement, then changed his mind, staring at her with an appreciation in his hazel eyes that seemed to come straight from his soul.

Dani could have said more. She could have told him that no parent knows what to do all the time. That nine-tenths of parenting entails gut instinct and keeping your fingers crossed and knowing that whatever you do, you've done it with love. For the time being, though, all she could do was look at him.

He cares about my son.

It was such a simple thing, it might have meant little to somebody else. But to Dani, who knew too well that genuine caring was a rare commodity, Sam's simple kindness was worth a king's ransom.

Timmy tried so hard to be grown-up for his mother, almost as if he sensed that she needed comfort as much as he. He'd cried when Charlie died, yes, but he'd recovered quickly, perhaps too quickly, becoming almost stoic about the hapless guinea pig. Tonight, though, alone with Sam, he'd felt the license to be nothing but a child, confused and angered and saddened by the loss of his pet. And Sam, bless him, had seen her boy's uncertainty and his need and sought to reassure him.

This must be what it's like to parent with a partner, she thought. Relaxing in the knowledge that someone else would pick up the baton if you dropped it must feel like sliding into a hot bath at the end of a long day. To rest against the cushion of someone else's confidence...

Except Sam hadn't been confident.

His gruff admission of uncertainty made Dani smile. Her voice rippled with candid appreciation. "Sam Mclean, I could kiss you for what you did."

He went absolutely still. The air between them whispered madly with electricity.

Another log crackled and dropped in the fireplace, spitting sparks into the hearth, and Dani flushed. "I mean, it was— I was..."

This time the glow in Sam's eyes had nothing to do with reflected firelight. "I like the way you put it the first time."

Moving slowly around the couch, he came to her side. His powerful shoulders gave the impression of strength and command, but the hand that reached out to touch her cheek was infinitely gentle.

And this, Dani concluded with a catch in her throat that was almost a gasp, *must be what it's like to be married to your lover.* Standing in the living room of a house redolent with the aroma of the onions you'd fried for dinner, echoing with the sound of piano music and adult conversation and a child's bedtime prayers, silent now except for your breath and that of the man standing before you. The same man who poured catsup on your roast beef hash and dried your dishes and made your heart race every time you looked at him.

Sam's hand slipped slowly from her cheek to her jaw to the nape of her neck. One more step forward brought him bare inches away, and he closed that gap with a hushed murmur. "Dani."

His were the first lips she'd kissed in years. It was better than she remembered. Much.

The kiss was light and clever, leaving her hungry for more.

She felt his fingers tighten on the back of her neck even as he lifted his head, and she knew that pulling away was not his first impulse, either. He wanted more as much as she.

Pulling away was, however, the smart choice.

Dani became aware of her heart slamming in her chest, beating in an insistent rhythm that echoed her thoughts. *What-now? What-now? What-now?*

Sam's thumb stroked her jaw.

Another log fell in the fireplace.

What would a man like Sam expect? She could feel the sexual heat vibrating between them. They lived in the same house. To ignore what was happening between them would be pointless and impossible. But to act on it?

.Dani knew that few people these days, male or female, required marriage or even the suggestion of it as a prelude to sex. The attic was private and discreet and had a double bed. They could become clandestine lovers and no one need ever know.

Unless her son looked for her in the middle of the night. Or her father noticed how their gazes held when she handed Sam the strawberry preserves in the morning.

A reluctant quiver ran through her. *Would* their gazes linger? Would their fingertips flirt? If they made love tonight, would passing the butter turn into a silent seduction tomorrow?

She shook her head. She'd traveled this road before, hearing whispers of forever in every murmured, "Scoot over, hon, my leg's falling asleep." She couldn't make the same mistake this time.

"I must be rustier than I thought."

The low, handsome rumble interrupted her musing.

Sam arched a brow. "If my kiss makes you frown, then I'm rustier than I thought."

Dani swallowed, bit her bottom lip and answered, "No. Your technique is…definitely intact. Not to worry."

They smiled at each other.

Sam felt only moderately reassured. Gut instinct told him there was definitely something unspoken in Dani's response. An implied, *Now why did I go and do that?*

He wanted to kiss her again, hard and fast and insistently enough to make her admit she'd kissed him because she wanted to, that in fact she'd love to do it again, right this minute. Heaven knew *he* wanted to.

Instead, he released her, letting his hand drop. The moment grew awkward and unfinished. Like a ball player running between second and third base, trying desperately not to be tagged out, they couldn't move forward and couldn't back up.

Maybe he would have kissed her again if he hadn't caught the flicker of sadness in her eyes before she glanced away.

"Dani, look at me." When she did, Sam reached inside for the courage to be honest. "I think you're wondering where we go from here. So am I. And I think you're remembering that I've got plans to leave after the first of the year."

He heard the tiny intake of breath that said she was surprised—and that he was right.

Inclining his head toward the couch, he requested, "Sit with me."

They perched side by side without touching. In an

effort to relax physically, Sam hooked an arm—the one not next to Dani—over the back of the couch. His fingers grazed a patch of worn upholstery. Bordering on threadbare in spots, the sofa would have to be replaced someday soon. Suddenly, swiftly, it occurred to him that in thirty-two years he'd never picked out furniture with a woman. He could see Dani shopping for couches and chairs, testing for comfort, looking at price tags. He could picture a man with her, arguing for leather, grumbling as she made him sit on yet another armchair, pulling her down with him when the salesman wasn't looking.

The image was so damn easy to see.

When Dani looked at him so sweetly and shyly, he wanted to take her in his arms again that very instant. His fingertips burned with the need to touch her.

"This is a new one for me." He shook his head.

"What?" Even that one word seemed like an effort for her. She was holding her breath.

"Saying to an employer what I'm about to say to you. Somehow I can't imagine telling the post commander I'd like to make love."

It took a moment for Dani to register what he'd just said and another moment to process it. Her response came slowly—a pleased, receptive smile.

Sam withdrew his arm from the back of the couch and shifted to face her. "I don't want to insult you. You hired me, I've been here a week...I'm not trying to take advantage of the situation." His gaze was as direct, as forthright as he could make it. "But I want to know you better. You're an attractive woman, Danielle Harmon. And I want to be with you more than I've wanted to be with any woman in a long, long time.''

Hope, desire, pure female satisfaction—the emotions curled through Dani's veins like smoke around a spire.

Wow. Wow, wow, wow! When Brian had walked out, he'd taken her confidence with him.

Sam just brought it back again.

Dani smiled. He was so close, she could have touched his cheek.

''Thank you,'' she said simply. ''I'm attracted to you, too.''

His expression didn't change, exactly, but it deepened. His eyes grew darker, his lips firmer. Dani felt a quiver of response deep inside.

''We haven't discussed the ad you put in the paper. *Your* ad, Dani.'' He paused, obviously expecting the same reluctance she showed the last time he mentioned it. ''I think we should talk about it now, don't you?''

Her heart gave a strong, quick thump. ''Okay.''

''As I understand it, you were looking for a permanent arrangement. Someone who could help you on the farm...and in the house. A partner. It makes sense.''

''It does?''

Sam nodded. His gaze traveled the living room, touching various points—the fire, the piano, bookshelves filled with pictures of Timmy and Pop. ''You're building something good here.'' His voice and expression were complimentary, but contemplative, too, almost gruff. He fixed his gaze on her again. ''The ad was a good thing. Don't regret it.''

She was regretting it less and less with each passing moment.

Words tangled with the bubble of excitement lodged in her throat. If he was saying what she thought he was saying...

"You think it was right that I advertised for a husband?"

His eyes grew dusky. When he brushed her cheek, she felt the roughness on the pad of his thumb. *From sanding my porch,* she thought. His voice was rough, too, as he answered, "I think it's just right."

Her breath wouldn't come. Never before in her life had she been so close to making one of her dreams a reality. It was a frightening, exhilarating, wonderful feeling.

Sam's presence here, his interaction with her family this past week had made one thing clear to her—man, woman, child—it was the simplest, most mystical, most primal of all human groupings. It was what she wanted. And she wanted it, she was growing more certain all the time, with Sam. She relished his kindness, admired his strength. She wanted to learn all about him. She knew already that he loved cabbage, hated peas, had infinite patience with others and little for himself. There would be so much more to discover, and she found suddenly that she couldn't wait.

Fighting her innate bashfulness, she pressed her cheek into his palm, then raised her hand and curled her fingers around his. Such strong, capable hands. A wondrous new softness settled inside her as she drew his hand away and glanced down, studying all the distinct lines and deep grooves.

"I went to a sweet sixteen party once. There was a palmist there. She told us our futures just by looking at our hands."

"Dani, I—"

"I got kind of interested in it for awhile." When their words overlapped, he let her continue. "I took a book on palmistry out of the library. I must have read Pop's hand a hundred times. For five cents a shot."

The lips she loved to sneak glances at curved upward, and Dani didn't need a palmist to tell her she would never get tired of making Sam smile. Feeling bolder than she had in a long time, she traced one of the lines on his hand. "You need more laughter," she said, arching a brow as she pretended to cull the information from his palm. "You take life very seriously."

As if to credit her words, his expression grew somber. "What else do you see?"

"Oh, lots of things. Your lines are unequivocal—long and clear. You're stubborn and don't change your mind easily."

"True enough."

"And here," she said, "this is the head line. You're more intellectual than creative, but you're very passionate."

"And can be very creative while passionate, which is probably more important."

She looked up swiftly to realize he'd been staring at her the whole time she'd been gazing down. Before she could resume her palmistry, he flipped his hand over, clasped her wrist and tugged her toward him.

When there was barely enough space between them for a whisper, when she could smell the faint musk of his cologne and his skin, he growled against her. "I want you. Can you read that on my palm?"

Dani trembled. "No." She shook her head. "In your eyes."

His gaze burned a path through her desire. "This isn't what you want," he said gruffly. Sam's touch was so firm and Dani's need so strong, she felt as biddable as a rag doll. "Any palm reader can tell you there's a world of difference between a woman like you and a man like me."

The corners of her mouth trembled as she looked at him quizzically. "I hope so."

He shook his head. "That's not what I mean. I don't want you to get hurt."

"I won't." His frowning hesitation made a frisson of doubt curl in her belly. Something was wrong. Sam's hands commanded her closer. His voice and expression warned her away.

"I'm not sure... I don't understand." Striving for a lightness she no longer felt, she asked, "Aren't you...applying to my original ad?"

Her voice and her smile were teasing, almost coquettish. By comparison, his solemnity seemed stark, uncompromising.

He hesitated before he spoke, and a world of regret was contained in that pause. "No." All the gentleness in the world would have been incapable of removing the hurt from his response, and he knew it. "I want you. Physically. Emotionally. But not—" a flash of abject pain crossed his face "not forever. That isn't something I can give." He put it baldly, refusing to lead her on. "That's what I was trying to tell you. I should have said it plainly before. If marriage is one of your prerequisites—" his gaze was steady as a rock "—I can't fulfill it."

Who said honesty was the best policy?

For several protracted seconds, the heartbeat pounding in Dani's throat was the only clue she had that she was still breathing. It seemed ridiculous to have this conversation while they were still physically entwined, so she inched her face back, moved her knee far away from his thigh, let the hand that had been reaching toward his shoulder lower slowly to her lap.

The only words that came to mind were a protest. *But I think I love you.*

Well, no use in saying that. *Dear Lord, don't let me say that.*

She sat in silence, longing to be four years old again, to believe that if she closed her eyes she would become invisible.

Sam let her draw away. He gave her the physical distance she needed but broke the silence with an angry oath. "This is my fault." He shook his head and swore again. "That was clumsy as hell. I'm—"

Dragging her voice from the pit of her stomach, where everything seemed to have settled, she told him, "No. Please, it's not all your fault, it was a misunderstanding, and—" She took a breath that shuddered. "I'm fine. Everything's fine. I—" She forced a laugh. "Well, I'm a *little* embarrassed. Okay, a lot. Gee, sex in the nineties, huh? Love it or hate it?"

Sam didn't answer. He watched her trying to put them both at ease and felt his heart break.

What the hell had he been thinking, standing in this room tonight, waiting for her to come back? He was a selfish bastard, wanting to hold and keep what he knew damn well he shouldn't even touch. What he'd told her was the truth. He had nothing to give. But that hadn't stopped him from wanting to take.

She was beautiful. Vulnerable and sweet, compassionate and sincere. Her fair, lovely face trembled with the effort to keep smiling. If she could see herself as he saw her now...

She sought once more to ameliorate their growing discomfort, this time by explaining. "When you said you thought the ad was a good idea—"

"It was a good idea." If nothing else, he would have her believe that. "Dani." He quelled the urge to take her in his arms, trying to soothe with words instead. "A man would have to be blind not to see that marriage is right for you. It is," he insisted strongly when it appeared she was about to disagree. "Creating a family, thinking about the future is exactly what you ought to be doing. So the ad's a good idea. For you. And for some lucky son of a bitch who'll know a good thing when he sees it. I'm just—"

With surprising calm, she finished the sentence when he faltered. "You're just not that lucky son of a bitch." She smiled.

"No." He looked at her a long, long while. "I'm not."

Chapter Nine

She should have asked him to leave.

Dani stood at the kitchen sink, her hand in the interior of a cavernous pumpkin, scowling mightily as she scooped out seeds.

Three nights ago Sam had told her in no uncertain terms that he was not interested in marriage or, for that matter, in a long-term commitment of any kind. Since then, in an effort to prove she was unaffected by and therefore emotionally detached from his response, Dani had spent so much time smiling her cheeks had gone numb.

Taking a spoon, she dug into the pumpkin's pulpy fiber, ripping it out and flinging it into a bucket of compost materials. Too bad she couldn't perform the same ministrations on her feelings for Sam.

Currently he was stomping around on her roof. He'd been up there over an hour, insisting that he needed to patch a worn spot today while the weather forecast predicted a dry day. How, she had asked, was he going to go up a ladder with an injured hip?

He'd taken the comment as a challenge. A look of fierce masculine pride had tightened his features, and the next thing Dani knew, he was helping himself up the ladder, albeit carefully, one rung at a time.

Now he was moving around up there, every footstep making the roof creak, every creak making her nerves shudder.

A tear rolled off the tip of her chin and plopped into the pumpkin. *No! No, don't start that again!* She sniffed loudly and shook her head.

For three days—and three nights—her treacherous mind had been determined to recall the most tantalizing images of Sam, replaying them over and over like a crazed VCR. How could she claim detachment when all she could think about was the way his hands had massaged her back...and the clean, comforting scent of him as he moved in close for their kiss...and the way her fingers itched to touch his strong, bristled jaw.

Scraping the seeds from the pumpkin, Dani groaned. Why were the unavailable men so relentlessly attractive?

Why were the attractive men so relentlessly unavailable?

Setting her jaw, Dani dug at the interior of the pumpkin like she was determined to purée it with her spoon.

Above her the roof creaked again. One, two, three steps... Silence. He'd stopped. She heard some scratching noises, then the sound of hammering.

Sam had gone into town yesterday to buy supplies

for the roof and had returned with wood shingles, a half pound of nails and a plastic toy hammer for Timmy. He showed the little boy how to hammer safely, then spent the better part of an hour watching him pretend to nail down every piece of furniture in the house. Now every sharp, rhythmic blow of the hammer reminded Dani that Sam was there on her roof, fixing her shingles and fixing his presence in their lives so securely that even after he left, even if she never saw him again, he'd still be here.

Somehow she was going to have to find a way to stop thinking about him.

The hammering ceased. *Creak.* He took a step. *Creak, creak.* And a couple more.

Dani hefted the pumpkin onto the chopping board and grabbed a cleaver, then started singing to cover the sounds of Sam's movement. If she couldn't hear him, maybe she would forget about him, at least long enough to make her pumpkin butter in peace. With that goal in mind, she decided to sing—loudly—beginning with her own rendition of "Edelweiss" from *The Sound of Music.*

"Edelweiss, edelweiss, I don't hear a thing..." She belted the lyrics as if she was Julie Andrews twirling on top of a mountain in Austria.

Creak. Creak.

"Small and white, clean and bright..."

Creak.

"Oh, how I love to sing. Blossom of snow, I don't even know—"

Creak.

"How I'm going to make it through the next month with that man..."

Creak, creak...zzshiiing!

Dani hushed. That wasn't a step—that was a fall. She listened, but there was no other sound.

Leaving the pumpkin and cleaver right where they were, she ran out the back door. She raced to the front of the house where Sam was working, then skidded to a halt as a string of swear words, far more colorful than her singing, rained down from the roof.

She looked up to see Sam clutching his thigh at the juncture of his hip. He was seated, his injured leg straight out in front of him as he forced expletives through his gritted teeth.

At least he was in one piece. "Are you all right?" Dani squinted at him.

The swearing ceased. Sam looked down but didn't answer.

"I heard you walking around up here," she said. "Then it sounded like you fell. What happened?" For some reason, that question seemed to irritate him.

"Nothing!" He growled the two short syllables.

"I think you should come down from there now."

"I'm not finished yet. Go back in the house, Dani."

So much for courtesy and politeness. Dani put her hands on her hips. "I will not," she said. "That roof looks icy. I think you should come down. You fell, didn't you?"

Sam's lips thinned. "No, I didn't fall. I slipped."

"Oh." Shading her eyes from the glare of the sun as it tried gamely to poke through a cloud, Dani hid a smile. Injured male pride made Sam surly as a bear. "I don't have insurance to cover slips. Of course, if you'd fallen, that might be another matter. I'll hold the ladder. Do you think you can make it down okay?''

His eyes narrowed dangerously. ''I've got more work to do.'' Sam pushed himself to his feet, but not without an effort. The grimace he couldn't hide reinforced Dani's determination to get him off the roof.

''You're done for the day,'' she said, realizing how good it felt to drop the strained politeness with which they'd been communicating for days.

Towering far above her, he cocked a brow. ''Says who?''

''Says me,'' she challenged. ''And I'm the boss.''

Sam mulled that over. Finally a corner of his mouth lifted in a small, enigmatic smile. ''Hold the ladder steady.''

She did, and couldn't deny a frisson of concern as he moved with obvious discomfort. As he reached the ground, she moved aside.

With his feet planted safely on terra firma, Sam turned to her. ''All right, boss. Now that you've got me down here—'' his eyes glinted ''—what are you going to do with me?''

She put him in a hot bath with a handful of Epsom salts, that's what she did.

Or rather, she ordered him into the bath, then made a hot toddy and carried it to his room while he was still in the tub. She set a saucer on the cup to keep the drink warm, then hurried out of the attic and to the kitchen before Sam could find her. She had to think, and her brain turned to mush when he was around.

He was flirting with her. Reading the message in

his eyes, Dani knew that he still wanted an affair, and the knowledge both exhilarated and dismayed her. An affair was a dead end.

Moreover, Sam could claim all he wanted to that he wasn't the family type. She didn't believe him. He liked being here with her and Timmy and Pop. She knew he did.

What's the truth about you, Sam Mclean? What secrets do you keep? Because I know you're hiding something.

Standing at the sink, lost in her thoughts, Dani wasn't aware that her father had arrived home until he said, "Well, if you aren't thinking about something pretty important, then I ought to take your pulse, 'cause you're awful still."

She looked over to see him grinning at her.

"Hi, Pop."

Gene entered and tossed a small stack of envelopes on the table. "Picked up the mail."

"Oh. Thanks." Dani started chopping again. At this rate, her pumpkin butter wouldn't be ready for canning until after New Year's.

Gene went to the fridge, took out a package of pressed turkey breast, a loaf of wheat bread, a jar of mustard and a gallon jug of milk. He made a thin sandwich, poured a tall glass of milk and returned all the fixings to the refrigerator.

"Well, now I know something's up," he said, "because I'm about to ruin my appetite for supper and you aren't saying a word. This is the third day in a row you let me snack. You keep this up and I'll start to think you don't care."

Gene spoke with his usual good humor, but his

gentle brown eyes watched Dani closely. "Anything you want to talk about?"

Tempted to confide that her feelings for Sam were growing each day, Dani realized when she looked into her father's eyes that he already knew. The concern she read in his tender expression made tears rise to her eyes, and she glanced away. What could Pop tell her that she didn't already know? Only leprechauns chased after pots of gold.

Smiling as she focused on her chopping, Dani shook her head. From the corner of her eye, she saw Pop's shoulders lift and fall in a silent sigh. Picking up his plate and his glass, he set off for the living room. He was at the door when Dani said quietly, "Don't ruin your appetite."

Turning to acknowledge the comment, Gene smiled. "I won't."

When Pop was gone, Dani set her cleaver on the chopping board, wiped her hands and glanced at the clock. Two. Timmy would be home any minute, laughing and chattering about his day, giving her the best reason in the world to focus on something other than her own thoughts. Until then...

A little chocolate wouldn't hurt.

Her own baking didn't tempt her too much, but in one of the bottom drawers of the kitchen cabinet Dani kept a stash of miniature Three Musketeers bars saved from Halloween for just this sort of emergency. It was definitely a two-bar day, so she grabbed a couple, took them to the table and leafed through the mail in an effort to distract herself.

Two mail-order catalogues, four household bills—just what she needed—and a flyer advertising a special on holiday hams. Dullsville. Dani unwrapped a chocolate, took a bite and skimmed through the rest of the envelopes. Christmas cards, a donation request from a mission in the city... She frowned. Two of the envelopes bore handwriting she didn't recognize, addressed to her post office box but with return addresses that were unknown to her.

In the upper left-hand corner of the first letter, the sender's name was listed as William Frank Donnegan. Curious, Dani opened the flap and extracted a letter handwritten on inexpensive beige stationery.

Dear Ma'am,

Am answering ad. Am thirty-six-year-old male, five foot ten, sound health, nice looks. Have never been married but am looking to settle down, kids okay. Have farm experience—tractor, crop rotation, etc. Hard worker and good with animals. If interested, please call...

Chocolate nougat clung like glue to the roof of Dani's mouth. Swallowing hard, she got up from the table, went to the sink and drew a glass of water, which she drank in three gulps.

Whoa.

Someone had answered her ad.

Someone who didn't use pronouns.

Staring at the letter as if she expected it to grow a head, four limbs and a torso, Dani rubbed her palms down the front of her jeans and returned ever so slowly to the table. Her hand shook as she reached for the other letter. Should she open it or leave it where it was? Should she stuff the envelopes into the garbage and pretend she'd never even conceived of an ad?

Curiosity, if nothing else, triumphed over her misgivings, and she opened the letter from James Tenney of Boise, Idaho, as she slid slowly into her chair.

Dear Miss,

I am writing in response to the ad you placed in the *County Tribune*. Given the personal nature of such an ad, I feel some uncertainty with regard to the content of this letter. After much deliberation, I have decided that a brief autobiography may be most helpful to you in screening potential candidates.

I am thirty-two years old with a degree in horticulture and agricultural sciences. I hope it goes without saying that I am a bachelor. In addition to a long-standing enthusiasm for organic farming, I have a special interest in odorless fertilization and hope to develop my own fertilizer for distribution on a large scale in the near future.

On a somewhat more personal level, I consider family to be the most important thread in our ''American quilt,'' and look forward to establishing a home with a woman of like mind. With regard to expectations, I do not require great beauty, but am rather slender myself and so would prefer a woman of slender or average build. I mention this only to avoid awkwardness in the future. Intelligence and an interest in current events are assets, as I believe I can offer the same.

If the forestated information is agreeable to you, please contact me at the phone number or address listed below.

Dani put a hand to her forehead. My Lord, now what?

She would have to respond to the responses. Her heart started fluttering like a flag in the wind. She wasn't ready for this. Come to think of it, being single wasn't so bad. She could arrange her bookshelf alphabetically and no one would mess it up. She could eat in bed, watch a late-late movie, raise her son as she saw fit. Why muck it up?

There was no *reason* to answer these letters.

"Hi, Gene. Short day?"

"Yup, thought I'd knock off early. You up for a game of Hold 'Em?"

"You bet. I've got a little work to finish, then I'll take you on, sir."

The voices that carried from the living room gave Dani perhaps the only reason she needed for answering those letters—to try to forget how perfectly Sam Mclean fit in her heart and her life.

Chapter Ten

Beth sat on the couch, her hand on her belly, her eyes hungrily scanning the letter Dani had just handed her. "You've gotten how many of these?"

"Eight." Lacing her fingers on her lap, Dani nervously twiddled her thumbs. "They started coming a few days ago. I wasn't going to do anything about them at first, but then I..."

Beth smiled. "Then you decided to get real. Because you finally realized that men don't grow like your organic squash around here." She eyed Carrie, who was seated on the other side of Dani, eagerly sifting through the letters on her lap. "See anything interesting?"

Carrie nodded. "I see three distinct possibilities. I think we should rule out the two who wrote from prison."

Beth's brows rose. "Before we find out what they were incarcerated for?"

Dani put her hands over her face. "Oh, I can't believe I'm even considering this!"

She'd called her friends yesterday after another letter had arrived. The more studiously she had tried to avoid Sam these past few days, the more consistently her thoughts had turned to him. Finally she'd decided to do whatever it took to get him off her mind. And a couple of the letters she'd received weren't half bad.

She hadn't known Sam long enough to truly love him, after all. It couldn't happen that quickly. So her obsession had to be about something else. Maybe she was simply ready to be a wife.

"I can't believe you didn't tell us about the ad before." Despite her bright-eyed interest, Beth managed a moment of affronted disappointment. "I thought we were your best friends."

"You are my best friends," Dani placated, "that's why I'm asking for your help now. And I explained why I didn't tell you before. I was too embarrassed."

"Well." Beth sighed dramatically. "I suppose we can overlook one teeny transgression—as long as you tell us every detail from now on."

"Yes, Dani, please do!" Carrie pleaded. "Nothing this exciting has happened here in ages."

"And I don't get cable," Beth added, "so don't leave out the juicy parts. Okay, let's get down to business. You want us to help you decide who wins the date-with-Danielle lottery?"

Dani groaned. "I haven't gone on a date in six years. I'm not sure I remember how to talk to a man."

"It's like riding a bike," Beth said. "You wobble

a little and then you're off. The question is, why isn't tall, dark and husky in the running?" No one had to ask whom she meant. "Does he know about your ad?"

Dani rearranged two parenting and family magazines on the coffee table. "Yes, he knows."

"She said with casual unconcern," Beth quipped. "Has he shown any interest?"

"No."

"Too bad." Carrie wagged her head, her tight blond bun stuck to the back of her neck like a bunny's tail. "He's *so* handsome."

Certain Beth would pursue the subject of Sam, Dani was amazed—and a bit disappointed—when her friend let the topic drop. "All right," Beth said, "we need to do two things. One, pick the men Dani will date—the best three would be a reasonable start, I think—and two, turn our lovely, shy caterpillar here—"

"Shy?" Dani protested, "I'm not—"

"—into a gorgeous, seductive Monarch butterfly."

"Seductive? Wait a minute, that's not what I meant when I said—"

"Carrie, you go through the letters first. Be picky. Rule out anyone who sounds like he hasn't seen a woman in awhile. That includes the jailbirds. We'll narrow the field down until we come up with the best three prospects, then rank them in descending order from Most Likely To Be a Hot Date to Don't Get Up, I'll Call Myself a Cab. While you're doing that, I will take a peek at Dani's wardrobe." She began the laborious process of lifting herself from the couch. "We may have to go shopping."

"Shopping?" Reflexively, Dani reached over to help her friend up. "I can't afford—"

"Why don't you put on a pot of tea, sweetie?" Beth patted Dani's forearm. "I could use a snack." She rubbed her swollen tummy. "Got any pimento loaf? I'm crazy for that stuff lately."

"No, I—"

"Okay, a macaroon. Whatever." She rubbed her palms together, then gave a sharp, commanding series of claps. The woman who could not be persuaded to focus if her life depended on it when they were working on the holiday bazaar was suddenly all business. "Come on, ladies...hustle!"

The fireplace crackled and danced with amber flames.

Timmy sat on the living room floor, running his dump truck around a group of trucks and cars, and Gene sat at the dining room table, shuffling a deck of playing cards with the skill of a man who could deal poker for a living.

Sam smiled in contentment.

That was a funny concept, contentment. What did it mean, exactly? That you were happy with what you were doing in the moment or that you were just happy, period?

And, Sam thought, *which one am I?*

Sometimes, living in the Harmons' house, he felt plain fantastic through and through. Times like right now.

"You a betting man this evening?" Across the table, Gene cocked a brow at his new card buddy.

As they'd been doing almost every night for the past week, Sam and Gene were about to engage in a two-man poker tourney that would break for dinner, then resume and go on until one of them called it quits.

Eyeing Gene with arch calculation, Sam nodded. "I feel lucky."

"All right." Grinning, Gene countered, "You pick 'em. Bottle caps or toothpicks?"

Sam pretended to have to think it over. "Toothpicks."

Opening the box of toothpicks they'd used last night, Gene divvied up the contents. Meanwhile, Sam took the deck and started dealing the first hand. He'd won high card earlier.

"Granpop, I'm hungry," Timmy called from the living room. "When are we having supper?"

"'Bout fifteen minutes, son. Your mom's got a stew in the Crock-Pot."

Sam shifted in the chair and tried not to wonder what Dani had been up to this past week. For several evenings in a row, she'd retired to her room soon after the kitchen was tidied. Why she disappeared so early in the evening remained a mystery, but Sam was fairly certain that whatever the reason, her friends Beth and Carrie were involved. They came to the house frequently.

Ever since the afternoon when she'd left the hot toddy in his bedroom—a gesture that suggested a degree of intimacy Sam liked—Dani had affected a new and distant cordiality that said clearly, "Hands off."

He'd been flirting with her that day. More than flirting, really. He had wanted to seduce her.

Apparently she'd gotten the message loud and clear and was volleying with one of her own—*No, thanks.* He wasn't altogether surprised. Nor was he altogether certain he would have gone through with a tryst had it been an option. Sam didn't make a practice of misleading women. Dani had made it clear she wanted someone who planned to stick around, and he wasn't that man, not by a long shot. It was a damned pity, too, because even now he wondered what those long, long legs looked like under the jeans she wore so well. And he wanted to see the dense red curls spill across his pillow like a river on fire.

Most of all, though, he longed to touch her, actually ached sometimes when he thought about holding her. He wanted to take every wonderful thing that was Dani and devour it, like a man who'd been half starved most of his life and had only just realized it.

What made this situation so frustrating was that lately he couldn't define his reluctance to stay. She wanted a husband. He wanted her. He knew it was impossible, but he wasn't sure why anymore. Sam knew only that the thought of staying—and, yes, damn it, he had thought about it—made his whole body sweat, made him half blind with a nameless, shaming panic that he would repeat past mistakes.

"Ante up," Gene commanded, and Sam tossed a toothpick into the pot.

The little wooden sticks smelled like cinnamon.

Leave it to Dani to create hominess, a sense of comfort and good feelings even in the tiny details.

With the holiday only two weeks away, she'd decorated the house with candles, hand-painted pinecones and little ornaments she'd pulled out of storage boxes. Sam couldn't remember when Christmas had felt so much like…Christmas.

Wondering if they opened their gifts on Christmas Eve or Christmas Day brought a smile to Sam's face. He could picture Timmy on Christmas morning, all tousled red hair and toothy grin, sitting near the tree in a sea of wrapping paper. He could imagine Dani just as clearly, making a big show of loving whatever Gene and Timmy had gotten her.

And he, what would he be doing Christmas morning? Opening gifts with the family, of course. There was a small pile of presents with his name on them already growing beneath the tree.

Sam played his cards and bet silently, content to let Gene do most of the commenting.

Two weeks. Every morning at breakfast Timmy asked, "How long until Christmas?" To a little boy, two weeks seemed an eon. Sam had bought Timmy a sled for Christmas. He intended to teach his buddy how to use it safely before he left.

"What are you smiling at? You got a card up your sleeve?" Gene peered at Sam over the top of the cards.

Sam nodded to the small pot of toothpicks. "No, but it'll cost you to find out."

Gene studied his cards. Watching him, smiling at the telltale rapid blinking that signaled Gene's pleasure with the hand he'd drawn, Sam considered the

Christmas gifts he'd chosen for the other man and hoped he'd be pleased. He'd bought Gene a bottle of fine cologne and an eight pack of playing cards, along with a set of chips and a handsome wood case to hold them. The only family member he hadn't purchased anything for was Dani.

He wanted to get her something special, something she would use or wear after he was gone. Perfume, perhaps, or a scarf? Without questioning himself too much, he accepted that it was important to him to get the right gift, and he didn't want to rush it. He wanted to get her something feminine, something that would mirror the way he saw her, feminine and earthy, with an air of innocence that was—

"Wow!"

Timmy's exclamation jerked his attention to the living room.

Breathtaking. Sam finished his thought with an openmouthed stare.

"Mommy, you look diff'rent!"

Only five, and already a master at the fine art of understatement.

"Well, thank you, I think." Dani laughed.

Holy Kamoly, she sure did look different.

Without realizing what he was doing, Sam laid his cards on the table face up, exposing his hand.

Man, oh, man, did she look different.

So much for jeans and full skirts. So much for innocent.

A dress—a very short dress—in deep brown velvet caressed her curves like a lover's hand. And, oh, what curves they were! Her breasts, creamy and full above the scoop neck, made Sam's thought processes slow down while his heart rate sped up. Her long, dancer's arms were encased in tight-fitting sleeves. The dress skimmed over her hips and across her stomach in a relaxed I-don't-know-I'm-sexy manner that drove most men wild—Sam could vouch for that. Also, now he knew what her legs looked like.

He wasn't sure he should stand.... On the other hand, he was too bothered to sit still, so he rose slowly, meeting and holding her glance when she looked up from talking to Timmy.

"Daughter, you are a picture." Gene spoke before Sam did.

Dani looked at her father and smiled nervously. "Think so?"

"Yes." This time Sam spoke first.

Dani fussed with an earring. She wore the long, dangly kind that tangled with a woman's hair when her style was loose and free...and curling and red and gorgeous. Suddenly Sam's throat felt too damn dry. He cleared it.

"What's the occasion?" His voice emerged raspy and too low.

She glanced at her father as if he had the answer. "Oh, I—"

"Mommy, can I kiss you?" Timmy stood at her side, craning his neck to look up.

You and me both, kid, Sam thought. *You and me both.*

Dani smiled at her son, so softly and sweetly, Sam was sure that if he kissed her now, he'd taste honey. "Of course, pup." She bent down, giving Timmy access to her smooth cheek.

Her skin was the color of the richest cream, her

cheeks the shade of summer apricots. Timmy put a hand on her shoulder very importantly, as if that gesture was much more adult than throwing an arm around her neck, and pressed his puckered-up lips to her cheek.

Dani didn't try to kiss him back. She looked at him seriously and said, "Thank you. I hope you enjoy your dinner tonight. I made the stew you liked on your birthday. Remember?"

Timmy nodded vigorously. "I'm hungry."

"Good." She stood.

Sam's eyes followed her. "You're not eating dinner?" he asked, a truly stupid question. Since when did she dress like this for dinner around the kitchen table? So where...

She opened the clasp of a purse the same chocolate brown as her dress, checked the contents and snapped the bag shut. She smiled brightly, stating the obvious. "I'm dining out."

Which told him exactly nothing.

Gene stared at him as if he knew exactly what the younger man was thinking.

I hope not, Sam thought, starting to sweat, *because I'm thinking it about your daughter.* And that thought made him wonder why Gene hadn't been surprised in the least when Dani came downstairs dressed like...like Julia Roberts at a Hollywood bash. Obviously, Gene had known she was going out. He might even know where and with whom. Sam felt affronted suddenly, a sensation that made him want to cross his arms over his chest. *So how come I'm the last to know?*

Where *was* she going, anyway? Was she meeting

her girlfriends? Sam frowned. She wasn't dressed to meet other women.

Checking a slim gold watch that circled her wrist, Dani said to her father, "The stew should be ready. I have a couple of minutes, I'll get Timmy—"

"Don't you be silly now." Gene got out of his chair. "Dressed like that, you're not supposed to serve other people. You let them wait on you tonight."

She laughed and rolled her eyes. "That'll be the day."

Somehow her casual comment reassured Sam. Maybe she was meeting her girlfriends.

"I'll dish up the food. Son," he called to Timmy, "you come to the table now."

Scrambling to his feet, Timmy raced into the kitchen after his grandfather. That left Sam and Dani and a room pregnant with tension. She stood at the door, her inherent grace overshadowed by the awkwardness of the moment.

Seeking to relieve her tension and trying to say something that would elicit the pleased, shy smile he'd seen when her father and Timmy complimented her appearance, Sam said, "Your father's right. When a woman looks like you, she should expect to be catered to."

She didn't smile. She didn't roll her eyes or laugh. Dani merely stared at him, her beautiful emerald eyes large and luminous, the expression in them wary, almost sad.

Sam didn't understand. She looked like she didn't believe him, or didn't want to. Yes, he'd kept his distance the past few days, but only because he was following her lead. If it had been up to him...

Why hadn't he asked her out? He should have thought of that before, even as a simple gesture—a thank you for giving him work, making him feel welcome.

He stepped away from the table. "Dani..." He felt awkward as hell, but something told him to ask now, before she left for the night. "I know my timing is—"

Ding-dong.

"Lousy..."

Both their gazes swung to the door.

Someone was picking her up. Sam's mouth grew dry suddenly. He sincerely hoped that the pregnant woman or the other one, the mousy one, was on the other side of that door.

Ding-dong.

"I have to answer the..." She gestured.

Sam nodded.

It wasn't the pregnant friend, and it wasn't the mouse.

"Hi, I'm Leslie."

It wasn't a woman. It was a man. Named Leslie.

Sam felt every muscle he possessed contract. On the threshold, carrying a bouquet of flowers, stood Dani's date for the evening.

"I'm Danielle," she introduced herself. "Please come in. Oh, how lovely!" Accepting the bouquet he thrust at her, Dani touched the petals of a rose the same soft pastel shade as her cheeks.

Danielle? Roses? *Leslie?*

"Thank you." Dressed conservatively in a dark

suit, pale shirt and tie, Leslie entered the living room. He smiled at Dani as his eyes roved over her. He didn't miss a turn.

Sam seriously considered picking him up by the scruff of his too-thin neck and booting him out the door. If there was one thing he hated, it was thin, pale, conservatively dressed men who smiled politely but couldn't keep their eyes to themselves. Guys named Leslie.

"Why don't you have a seat?" Dani gestured to the couch. "I'll put these in a vase. And may I get you anything to drink, Leslie?"

Sam scowled fiercely. The way she said his name, it sounded...not too bad.

"We have dinner reservations at seven," Leslie said, checking his watch by flicking his wrist and giving it a little shake as if the timepiece didn't work properly.

"Oh. How long will it take to get to the restaurant?"

"About a half hour. I don't like to drive quickly with the roads slick."

Dani bestowed an approving smile.

"Where are you going?" It was the first time Sam spoke and the first time Leslie realized that he and Dani were not alone. Sam smiled, relishing the other man's surprise.

"Oh, I'm sorry! This is Sam." Dani made the perfunctory introduction, elaborating, Sam noticed, only when Leslie looked curious. "Sam is my employ—" She stumbled over the word employee, and Sam folded his arms smugly. They were more to each other than employer-employee. *Yeah, that's right. Don't look too comfy over there, Leslie, boy.*

"Sam works for me," Dani finished, eliciting an Ah-I-see nod from Leslie and a scowl from her workman. "I'm going to the kitchen for a vase. I'll just be a minute."

Turning his head, arms still folded, Sam watched her walk into the kitchen in her high-heeled pumps. He watched her legs and he watched her tush, then he turned to Leslie—slowly, casually, a man who knew he'd been caught ogling his employer's bottom and didn't care.

"Blind date?" he asked Leslie, allowing a small, alpha-male smile.

"Well…" Leslie frowned. Not sure he should be speaking to the help about such things? "I suppose…in a manner of speaking."

"What do you do, Leslie?"

"For a living?" Leslie adjusted the knot of his tie. "I'm employed in Boise. I work for the *Tribune*."

"The paper? Are you a reporter?"

"No." Leslie cleared his throat, a nervous gesture. "A typesetter."

"Hmm." Sam's mind worked furiously. Who had set them up? And how good a match was it? A typesetter at the *Tribune*. That sounded like—

Sam's thoughts skidded to a halt. A typesetter on the *Tribune* sounded like someone who had read Dani's ad! Man-o-mighty, was that what was going on here? Was this nervous shmoe a husband candidate? Had she really gone through with that harebrained, stab-in-the-dark plan to find a mate?

Feeling the tension on his forehead increase, his

brows nearly meeting in the middle, Sam stared malevolently at the other man. No, no way. She wouldn't have, not this close to Christmas. This was a time for family, for staying home with people you knew.

"Here they are, and they look lovely." Dani came in, holding the vase of mixed flowers in front of her. She set them on the dining table, then moved into the living room. Toward the shmoe.

"Where are you going?" Sam asked. He sounded like her father. Where was Gene, anyway? Both Dani and Leslie looked at him like they were surprised he considered that information any of his business, and he glared.

Damn straight, it was his business. Someone had to know where they were heading, for how long and when they expected to return. This guy was a stranger she'd met through a newspaper. Precautions had to be taken.

"What's your license plate number?"

"Sam!"

"I beg your pardon?"

Apparently neither of them cared for this question, either. Sam felt himself grow obstinate. He looked at Dani, gorgeous and sexy and dressed for a hot date, and addressed his next comment to her.

"Does your father know where you're going?"

"Sam—"

He held up a hand. "Excuse me, but this is a blind date—or am I mistaken?" He divided his glance between the two of them, then settled on Leslie with a smile guaranteed to chill any steamy notions the man might have. "I'm an officer in the United States

Army when I'm not working for Dani. I do things by the book, so you'll have to bear with me." *Or get out*, the broadened smile implied. "This is the nineties and a few precautions are in order. I'm sure you agree, Les, having Dani's best interests at heart, like I know you do. So I'll get a pen to take down that information." He stepped toward the kitchen. "Won't be but a minute. Oh, and why don't you get your driver's license out in the meantime. That ought to speed things along. After all, we want to get you to the restaurant in time for your reservation."

Chapter Eleven

All right, so he'd made an ass of himself.

Sam stared out the window at the dark night and swirling snow and recalled Dani's furious glare as she walked out the door with her date. *You're fired,* the look seemed to say, and even though Sam had Leslie's driver's license number, his address and the name of his insurance company on a slip of paper, he didn't feel very triumphant as the front door closed.

"Home by eleven," Dani had told him between her clenched teeth. It was almost that now. Gene had retired for the night over an hour ago after a game of poker that was singularly unsatisfying. Sam hadn't been able to focus his attention at all. Gene, on the other hand, had exhibited admirable concentration. Apparently he'd had a change of heart about his daughter's personal ad. When Sam stated that Leslie had an evasive gaze, Gene merely shrugged, commenting with typical nonchalance, ''Got to read the book before you know the story.''

Sam grimaced in distaste. If he was smart, he would get away from this window before she came home and saw him standing here like some testosterone-injected duenna. What was he doing save for humiliating himself and irritating the hell out of her?

Ploughing restless fingers through his dark hair, he noted tangentially that it had grown out since he'd left active duty. He'd have to get it cut before he left for Florida.

Florida. Every time he thought about leaving, his body burned as if he were on fire inside. He couldn't find a comforting thought tonight. Visions of staying, of going—they were all the same, all agonizing. Why? Sam shook his head. He didn't understand himself, and he found that aggravating.

Headlights bobbed and dipped as a car turned up the rutted road to the house. Without stopping to think, Sam backed away from the window, letting the curtain drop into place. Uh-oh.

Moving quickly, he turned on the TV, then jumped onto the couch in a fully reclined position. He settled himself as if he was sleeping, bolted up with a second thought, grabbed a magazine from the coffee table and placed it open over his chest. Then he turned his face toward the back of the sofa and waited. And waited...

And waited.

He heard the car pull up, heard one door slam and then another. He lifted his head, listening. Mr. Dream Date would walk her to the door, of course, but would she invite him in? If she did, she'd be beyond furious when she found Sam here. If he got up now—

Uh-oh, too late! Her key turned in the lock. Swiftly, he flopped his head down and started snoring as the door opened and Dani walked in.

"Thank you, Leslie. I had a wonderful time."

She sounded so sincere, Sam had to force himself not to peek over the back of the couch. There followed a low male murmur that Sam couldn't make out above his own snoring, and finally the soft closing of the front door. He hadn't heard any kissing sounds.

The wood floor creaked beneath the carpeting as Dani moved around. Sam made a big, yawning production of awakening from his nap.

"Ah—" he stretched, glanced around as if he wasn't quite sure where he was, then noticed her and smiled. "Oh, hi. What time is it?"

"Ten to eleven." *Pleased t' see ya* would not properly describe her countenance at that moment. *Get off my sofa, you bumble-mouthed toad head* would have been more accurate.

Lowering his feet to the floor, Sam considered his options. Dani's visage was stern, her body rigid. All right, so perhaps now was not the best time to ask prying questions about the success of her date. It might, however, be a good time to apologize for being a jerk.

Rubbing his brow, Sam turned toward her, mouth open to grovel. She was staring at him like a nun in an overstarched wimple.

Hmm. Perhaps now wasn't a good time to apologize, either.

He could let it go till tomorrow, let her unwind a little first. Slapping his palms together, he stood. "Well, guess I'll hit it."

"Don't—you—move!"

"Huh?"

For a man who'd spent much of his adult life barking orders at others, Sam found that he was easily cowed by a five-foot seven-inch woman with flaming red hair, a figure to die for and a real good reason to be angry. Well, maybe not cowed, exactly. More like fascinated.

She was furious with him. Damn, she was stunning when her eyes blazed and the color flared in her cheeks. The line of her jaw was gorgeous, too. He could see more clearly how strong and defined it was when it was clenched.

"How dare you embarrass me like that?" Her voice was dusky, vibrating, held low by strict control. "I wanted to make a good first impression on Leslie."

Sam let a grunt stand as his response. She'd taken off her coat. Did she have any idea what a body like hers in a dress like that did to a man's senses? If Leslie hadn't been made half stupid by the sight of her, then his sexual persuasion had to be questioned.

"You made a terrific first impression." Sam sounded like he'd just downed a pint of whiskey. The way he felt, a stiff shot of something numbing didn't sound like a half-bad idea.

His compliment took some of the heat out of Dani's ire. She uncrossed her arms, plucked at her sleeve. "Really? How could you tell?"

"It's a man thing."

"Oh. Well, good."

"Did you enjoy the date?"

Sam figured he had to be either really stupid or really desperate to ask a question to which the only answer he wanted was no. A scowl gathered across his brow even before she responded.

Dani brushed imaginary lint from her skirt. An answer—the one she'd rehearsed silently in the car all the way home—hovered on the tip of her tongue. *Wonderful time.* Just like she'd told Leslie.

A faint queasiness rolled in her tummy, a sensation that had nothing to do with dinner.

Poor Leslie had been ready to call it a night before they'd even reached the end of the driveway. Probably before they'd stepped off the porch. Sam had intimidated him thoroughly.

It had become clear to Dani early in the evening that she and Leslie were not suited. She had barely drawn five words from him by the time they finished the salad course. Still, she'd told Sam she would be home around eleven, and darned if she'd been willing to show up one minute earlier! So she had nursed her coffee until it was cold, then asked for a fresh cup, and she'd ordered dessert after Leslie had told the waiter no thanks. In fact, her date had been so eager to cut the evening short, he'd already taken out his wallet! Her first time back in the dating saddle had been a disaster, no doubt about it.

Worst of all, she'd compared Leslie to Sam all evening. The thought of having to go on two more of these blind dates was chilling. She didn't want to sit with a stranger and wonder if he had the patience to answer a five-year-old's endless questions, or whether she'd be able to feel him staring at her when she played the piano. With Sam, she already knew.

When he encouraged her to follow through on her ad, she'd been absolutely convinced he was telling her that he was not interested. But if that was the case, why had he reacted so negatively to Leslie tonight? Why was he scowling right now?

Sam was inherently protective, yes, but that wasn't a big brother's look he'd given her when she'd entered the living room tonight. He had looked at her exactly the way a woman wants to be looked at by a man. He admired her, desired her—she could feel it. And unless she was very, very mistaken, the connection between them was more than merely sexual.

Even now the look in Sam's eyes was deep and multilayered. A surge of frustration made Dani's stomach and chest tighten. *Why can't it be you?*

She answered Sam's question with less fabrication than she'd originally intended. "I had a...fine time."

"Fine? Not much of a recommendation."

She shrugged. "Not much of a time."

He exhaled, long and slow. "I'm sorry."

"Are you?"

"Not about the date. About the way I reacted." He shook his head. "We both know I didn't have any right to question him like I did."

"Well. You were being cautious."

"I was being a jerk." There was a couch between them. Sam walked around it, never once taking his eyes off Dani.

"My friends checked him out before I agreed to the date," she said, whispering the words as Sam came closer. "Where he works and lives... He seems like a very nice—"

Sam put two fingers to her lips. "Shh." His voice was hushed and sandy. "I don't care about him. Only you."

With reverence and a gentleness that nearly brought tears to Dani's eyes, he slid his fingers into her hair, through the waves hanging long and free. His expression was exquisitely serious. "There isn't a man you could bring in here who would be good enough for you. Not in my eyes. But then I'm biased, Dani. I think I may be hopelessly biased."

She forgot to breathe as he curved a hand around the nape of her neck. He took a step closer and then another until they could feel the energy from each other's body, until only his whisper came between them. "One kiss." Sam arched a brow, searching her face. "All right?"

No, the answer screamed through her even as she lifted her head. *One kiss and I'll be lost. One kiss and I'll never be able to forget you, I know it, not as long as I live.*

For good or bad, Dani's heart spoke more loudly than her intellect. Her soul spoke loudest of all. "Yes."

Sam didn't waste a moment once he sensed the strength of her desire. Lips met and opened. He tasted her as if she were fine wine. Dani raised her hands to Sam's shoulders, her fingers spanning muscles so strong and well-formed that the feel of them sent chills down her spine. When their mouths parted to allow a breath, he trailed kisses as hot as lava, a molten, unbroken river of them, down her neck and onto her collarbone. Breathing in the scent of him, Dani decided he smelled like all the things she loved best about Idaho—the cleanness, the woodsy strength, the simplicity.

He kissed the little notch in the middle of her collarbone, and she felt her pulse leap beneath his lips. His thick, coarse hair brushed her neck and chin. Dani leaned back, floating, falling, coming alive and dying a little in his arms. A small half-sad, half-delighted smile brushed her lips. *And all the king's horses and all the king's men couldn't put Dani together again.*

As she melted into him, Sam couldn't believe the feeling, how strong and powerful and right it was. If there was another woman in the world right now, he didn't know about it, didn't want to know. Dani. The whole world was Dani, and at this moment the world was a damn fine place to be.

Working his way up her neck, he pressed a nibbling kiss onto the corner of her mouth and felt her smile. He pulled away just enough to look at her. "What?"

"You said *one* kiss." Her tone teased.

He grinned, feeling cocky and possessive and very much a man who knew what his woman liked. "You want me to stop?"

Dani trailed her fingers down the front of his shirt. "I think this is one of those times when what I want may not be what's good for me."

Sam knew she was asking a question as much as making a statement. Her beautiful green eyes were wide and ingenuous, the lashes spiky, making her look almost painfully innocent. The words he wanted to say caught in his throat.

He reached for her hands, drawing them to his chest, holding on too hard, but he needed her strength to find his own. This was when the panic came, this moment when he began dreaming of a future that included a woman like Dani and—he could barely let himself think it—a boy like Timmy.

You'll be safe with me. I will be good for you. Both of you. That was what he wanted to tell her, what he wanted to believe himself. Oh, God, how he wanted to take a chance—one chance, one time, with this woman—and make it come out right.

"I know it's too soon to talk about tomorrows." Dani must have mistaken his hesitation for reluctance, because she sought to fill in the blanks. "Maybe if I was alone, if it was only me, I wouldn't have to..." She shook her head. "That's not true." Gently, she pulled her hands from Sam's grasp. "I think I can say what I have to better if we're sitting down."

They moved to the couch, together but not touching. Sam waited for Dani to begin, because he sensed she wanted it that way. More than anything, though, he would have loved to take her in his arms and erase the concern from her lovely face. His body was still vibrating with the passion they'd ignited.

"I was in love with Timmy's father," she began. "I didn't have a fling. I was in love. I thought it would last. When I found out I was pregnant with Timmy, I got scared—we hadn't talked about children—but I was excited, too. All my life I'd pictured myself with a family." Even now her eyes glowed with the image. "And I thought that if you loved someone and he loved you..." She shrugged, transferring her gaze from the wall opposite them to her hands. Sam could feel the difficulty with which she continued this conversation. "Brian wanted me to have an abortion." She whispered the word. "When I said no, he told me he wouldn't be involved with the baby. I kept seeing him anyway. That ought to give you an idea of how naive and desperate I was. I actually thought he'd come around. Until I found out he was seeing a woman who worked in the same office we did." Her forehead crimped with the pain and humiliation of self-deception, but she faced Sam squarely. "So now when a man tells me he's not the family type, I believe him."

The words fell like a hammer on Sam's heart.

When Dani first started her story, outrage had filled him, fury at Timmy's father for being so selfish and immature he'd hurt a woman whose only mistake had been to trust him.

Then the realization struck. *A man so selfish and immature... A man who couldn't commit....*

How could he condemn Brian for possessing the same selfish egoism Sam had himself? They had commited different crimes, but he and Timmy's father shared the same fatal personality flaw.

When they first sat down on this couch, Sam had thought, *I'll tell her. I'll tell her all of it and ask her to take a chance on me. I could put my past to rest and walk into the future with this woman.*

But now, after all that Dani had shared, he believed he knew exactly how she would react to the story he had to tell.

Twelve years ago Sam had slept with the daughter of his post commander—recklessly, irresponsibly and without love. When she got pregnant, Sam didn't run, not right away. He married Candace, proving what a responsible, upright guy he was.

Even now, his twisted sense of honor made him cringe. He'd married her—and hadn't paid her a moment's attention after the wedding, preferring to focus all his energies on his military career. The more Candace had complained, the more Sam had justified his absence from their house and their marriage. As for her pregnancy—

A lancelike pain, as physical as if he'd been stabbed with a knife, cut through his stomach. The prospect of becoming a father had terrified him so, he'd all but ignored his wife's pregnancy, and that's when he realized a man didn't have to leave physically to run away. At six and a half months Candace went into premature labor—on their living room floor. She'd barely made it to the phone to call a neighbor. Sam, when they located him, had made it to the hospital only in time to see his daughter struggle to take her last breaths. Candace had told him she never wanted to see him again as long as she lived.

Sam was no family man.

He'd been born to people who didn't know the meaning of the word, and apparently the sins of the father had been passed to the son.

"You've been up-front from the start," Dani continued with a tentative smile. "I appreciate that."

"I—"

"Please." She held up a hand. "Let me say what I have to, Sam, because this isn't easy for me, and I—" Tears gathered in her still-lake eyes, making them shine in the firelight. She swallowed hard, then continued. "Your being here is confusing to Timmy.

It's confusing to me. What I'm going to say is unfair, I know it. But I can't pretend that everything is fine when it's not. My son thinks you hang the moon, and I—''

The tears she could no longer hold back spilled slowly onto her cheeks. Using both hands to wipe them away, she forced herself to continue. ''I want you to leave. I thought I put that ad in the paper for Timmy's sake. I didn't think I even wanted a relationship again, but I was wrong. I did it for me, too. You must think I'm crazy, first the ad and now this.'' She waved to indicate the two of them and her tears. ''I've never felt more mixed up in all my life, but there are a couple of things I realized for sure tonight. I want to be a wife and a best friend, not just someone's lover. And—'' she looked at him with all the strength she could muster and with the vulnerability she couldn't hide ''—I can't pretend I don't care about someone when I do. It'll be too hard for me if you stay.''

Oh, God. Sam bunched his hands into fists to keep from touching her.

She wanted him to leave. The knowledge snaked through him like a rusty coil. He should have been grateful that she'd said it before he was forced to, but all he could think was *Leave. Leave? Before Christmas. Before the mistletoe was hung.*

Before desire could build to passion and passion to something stronger and more impossible to forget.

He clenched his fists harder. Oh, who was he kidding? He didn't need more time to know Dani was his chance to love completely. And now he was being given a choice: Stay and take a chance with a woman who touched the soul he thought he'd lost long ago, or leave. It should have been easy.

For an instant, he thought he would do it—ask to stay, beg if he had to. But then it came, a feeling he recognized at once, the same bitter, gut-cramping fear he'd carried deep inside—mostly buried—for years. It swelled even as Sam fought against it, a strange stark terror that left no room for reason. And no room for hope. This kind of fear did not belong in the heart of a husband and father. This was the kind of fear that, in battle, made men AWOL. Out of battle, it made them run, period.

Sam looked into Dani's eyes and wondered, not for the first time, at the irony of a life that would offer him a family without first giving him the courage he needed to love them as they deserved.

As his gaze locked with hers, the need to touch her made his fingers tremble. He wanted so much to hold her, to savor for just a moment what he wished he could claim for a lifetime.

The words, *I'm sorry,* strained for release until his throat was sore, but he was afraid that if he said them once, he would wind up uttering them over and over and embarrass them both.

In the end, Sam simply closed his eyes, sick with shame and disgust, and gave Dani the only response he could summon: one slow, aching nod that said, *Yes. I'll leave before Christmas.*

Chapter Twelve

Tightening bolt G on the sled he was assembling for Timmy's Christmas present, Sam took a brief glance at the clock on the mantel. Eleven forty-two. Plenty of time to clean up, hide the sled and leave a note telling Gene where to look for the gift. Sam would be out of here and on the road, he estimated, by one. He was already packed.

After the heightened emotion of last evening, he'd tossed and turned in his bed until the early hours of morning. He'd forgotten to set the alarm, slept through breakfast, then came downstairs to a silent, empty house and a note informing him that Dani and her father had gone into Boise to make deliveries and pick up kitchen supplies.

With the wrench in his hand, he rubbed his knuckles across his forehead. Lousy morning.

Setting the sled on the floor, Sam leaned on it to test its durability. Solid. It would last Timmy many years.

And Sam wouldn't be here to see one of them.

Tossing the wrench into an open toolbox, Sam pictured Timmy's face when he saw the sled on Christmas morning. Then he pictured Dani bundled into her winter coat, her glorious red curls bursting like firecrackers from beneath her wool cap, smiling and laughing as she showed her son how to sled.

Sam had awakened this morning with such a desire to explain himself to her. To tell her *why* he would be a failure as a husband and father...and to let her talk him out of it.

He shook his head. Selfish, selfish. He would not allow himself to do it. For once, Sam Mclean would take the high road. After he left, Dani would find the man she deserved, somebody who wasn't carrying so much excess baggage that left no room in his arms for a wife and son. But the man she chose had damn well better be good enough for her.

Collecting the cardboard sled box, assembly instructions and bits and pieces of packing material, Sam took the mess out to the trash can. He returned chilled to the bone after only a minute or two outdoors. The weather was changing fast. This morning's mild gray sky was blustering now and spilling snowflakes in a steady stream.

According to Dani's note, her friend Carrie would pick Timmy up at school today, then babysit until Gene and Dani got home. There was nothing for Sam to do, really, except leave.

He hid the sled, placed the note for Gene and grabbed his gear. When he glanced back into the attic bedroom, it looked as empty and impersonal as he'd first found it.

Heading to his car, he tossed his duffel bag in the back seat and slammed the door, then heard the gritty crunch-crunch of another car rolling up the gravel drive.

An old green Dodge Dart pulled to a jerking stop next to his sedan. Dressed in a wool coat two sizes too large for her skinny frame, Carrie got out of the vehicle and hovered, torn, it seemed, between smiling nervously at Sam and mothering her passenger, a very tired, very grumpy-looking Timmy.

Sam lifted a brow as the child listlessly got out of the car and trudged toward the house.

"School let out early because a storm is coming." Carrie reached across the seat for the backpack Timmy had forgotten and twisted the straps with worried fingers. "And Timmy is sick."

"Am not," Tim grumbled.

Sam met him on the porch steps, crouched down to the boy's level and placed a hand on his forehead. It was warm, he thought, and a little clammy. Timmy was staring disinterestedly at his feet. "So what's wrong if you're not sick?" Sam asked gently.

"Don't feel good."

Hurrying to the door, Carrie used the key Dani had given her and ushered Timmy inside. "I didn't bring a vaporizer. Oh, dear, I hope Dani has one. And a strong rub. Everything will be fine, I'm sure. We can soak toast in milk for supper." She crossed the threshold muttering to herself. A moment before she closed the door, she remembered Sam and exclaimed, "Oh! Are you coming in—" her eyes bugged as if that prospect concerned her a lot more than finding a vaporizer "—or are you going?"

Frowning, Sam gestured toward the house, into which Timmy had already disappeared. "What do you think is wrong with him?"

"A winter cold. Nothing serious." Carrie offered a bright, toothy smile. "Mustn't be caught unprepared though."

Sam stood irresolute. He wondered what, if anything, Dani had told her friend about the two of them, but he was more concerned about leaving when Timmy didn't feel well. After all, what kind of father left when—

A sharp pain stopped that thought in its tracks. Fathers didn't leave when their kids were sick. Fathers didn't leave, period. *You're not his father.*

"I'm going." The words sounded guttural, like he'd dragged them up from his boots.

Nodding as if she was a bird with a worm in her mouth, Carrie closed the door without another word.

Sam forced himself to turn and walk down the porch steps. He forced himself to get into his car and turn the key in the ignition. Then he forced himself to forget that he hadn't wished Timmy a Merry Christmas.

Hunching her shoulders against a biting wind and darts of icy hail, Dani raced from car to phone booth, gratefully closing the folding door behind her. Rarely had she felt so frozen inside, but she wasn't altogether sure the weather was responsible.

She'd been lousy company for Pop today as they completed their last round of deliveries before Christmas. She'd barely been able to summon two words of conversation all day. Poor Pop had resorted to listening to Christmas carols punctuated by heavy static on the radio.

Lifting the pay phone receiver and using her teeth to tug the mitten off her other hand, Dani punched zero and her home number, then waited morosely for a disembodied voice to tell her to use her calling card or "press zero for an operator now." It seemed grossly insensitive of the phone company to use a mechanical voice even on the day before Christmas, but then it was a cruel, impersonal world.

Dani let her eyelids close briefly. Scrooge couldn't out-humbug her today.

She'd repeatedly gone over last night in her mind while Pop drove.

Maybe if she'd asked Sam point-blank to stay.... If she hadn't been so damned determined not to get hurt again.... There was no doubt about one thing, she'd jumped the gun big-time when she'd assumed Sam wanted the same things she did.

Generally, she liked to pretend that Pop was the old-fashioned one in the family, but the truth was, all her life she had dreamed of family the way it looked on TV during the fifties. Laura Petrie had Rob; Lucy had Ricky; even Ethel had Fred. And everything they did centered around home, children, neighbors. Each other.

Gripping the phone receiver tightly, Dani followed the instructions to enter her card number, then took a breath so deep, it hurt. Her mother had died long ago, but Dani never forgot—would never forget—how it felt to awaken to warm, spicy breakfast smells, to lie safe and indescribably comfortable in her bed while she listened to her mother puttering around the kitchen, discussing the day ahead with Pop. The memory of their mingled voices flowed as sweet as honey through her veins. They'd laughed together so often. She could hear the rhythm of their morning murmurs now. They'd giggle...get quiet... giggle again. Dani wanted that intimacy with some-one. With Sam.

She could picture him pulling her onto his lap in the morning when she walked by the table on her way to the stove. He'd nuzzle her neck and she'd dot jam on his nose, and they'd have to struggle to com-pose themselves when Pop and Timmy came in for breakfast. Yes, she could picture that. She'd been picturing it too darn much.

Counting three rings on the other end of the line, Dani curled her fingers around the cradle of the pay phone. Hope was a treacherous thing. It beckoned; it teased. And the moment you stopped resisting— bam! Right between the shoulder blades—that one-of-a-kind pain reminding you that dreams came at a price.

The phone rang a fourth time, and Dani realized her heartbeat was accelerating. She expected Carrie to answer...but that's not what she hoped for.

She hoped Sam had changed his mind and was in her kitchen right now, eating the tamale pie she'd left for dinner and chatting with her son. And think-ing about her.

Carrie answered on the fifth ring.

Dani's pulse slowed. After a brief exchange of hello's, she asked Carrie about Timmy. ''Is he run-ning you around much? You sound out of breath.''

"I just ran in from his room. He's in bed with a little cold."

"A cold? Does he have a fever?"

The line filled with static, through which Dani barely understood Carrie say that Timmy had a slight fever, but was comfortable...or coughing. Dani couldn't tell. "Carrie, I can't understand you. Did you say he's coughing?"

"What?" Carrie's voice crackled over the line like bacon frying. "I can't hear you."

"Carrie, is Timmy coughing? Because sometimes when he coughs badly, the cough syrup doesn't help and—"

"What? I can't hear you!"

"What? Carrie, hang up. I'll call you again."

This time, however, Dani couldn't get through at all, and the operator confirmed that the lines were down. Dani ran back to the car and relayed the news to Pop. The storm was obviously getting worse. They were still two hours out of town and probably should have stayed at a motel.

"But you remember that flu he had last winter, Pop? He coughed so hard he could barely breathe." Dani couldn't keep the worry out of her voice.

Gene nodded, his sage eyes evaluating what he could see of the dark sky through a hail-sprinkled windshield. It was starting to snow.

Dani frowned at the fat, swirling flakes. "We probably won't make it before the roads close anyway."

Turning the key in the ignition, Gene threw the car into drive. He nodded at his daughter. "Nothing I like more than a challenge."

* * *

What was typically a two-hour drive back to the farm took much longer. It was well after dinner when Gene pulled the car up the drive, and if he hadn't had the foresight to carry chains, they'd still be in Boise.

Despite her attempt to stay awake and to keep her father company, Dani had fallen asleep an hour ago and came awake only as he cut the engine.

"Are we there?" she mumbled groggily, lifting her cheek from the seat back. Rubbing the side of her face, she looked around to gain her bearings and frowned. "Whose car is that?"

"Don't know."

Dani recognized Carrie's ancient Dart, but the vehicle next to it was unfamiliar to her. Sam's car was nowhere in sight.

Curiosity warred with disappointment and fatigue as she fitted her key in the front door lock. It looked like all the lights were still on downstairs.

The moment she opened the door, warmth and aromas beckoned her. Cocoa and cinnamon and... something else. Gene edged past her when she hesitated in the doorway.

"Well, I'll take two orders," he joked to Carrie as she set a stack of cinnamon toast on the table.

Carrie looked up and clasped her hands together. "Oh, thank goodness!" Relief flooded her face. "I thought you must have stopped for the night, but Dr. Naditch said—"

"Dr. Naditch?" Dani stared at the salt-and-pepper haired man who sat at her dining table. Though he had been the family's doctor since Dani had moved to Idaho, Dr. Naditch had never made a house call. A rush of adrenaline jolted her tired body. "What's wrong?" She took two quick steps toward the doctor, who swivelled in his chair to deliver a pacifying smile. "Is Timmy worse? Is it that same cough he had before? How high is his fever?"

Before Dr. Naditch could answer, the patient in question called out, "Aunt Carrie, the caramel's burning!"

The swinging door that separated kitchen from dining room squeaked on its hinges as Timmy barreled through. "It's bubbling real fast. Mommy never lets it— Hi, Mommy!"

Dani looked from the doctor to her son. Dressed in his footed pajamas, Timmy appeared wide awake. "Why aren't you in bed?" she asked, moving quickly to put a hand on his forehead.

"Probably because he's not sick." Gene smiled.

Timmy scampered over to his grandfather. "Granpop, me and Carrie's making caramel apples."

Gene arched a brow. "Doctor's orders?"

"As good as medicine for what ails you." The country doctor grinned.

"What *does* ail him?" Dani stood with her hands on her hips. "He doesn't feel hot."

"He's fine." Dr. Naditch took a sip of hot cocoa. Chocolate foam lined his upper lip. "That is, I assume he's fine." He smiled at Timmy. "I haven't examined him. Do you need an examination, young man?"

"Uh-uh!"

Dani looked at Carrie in mounting confusion.

"He's fine." Carrie bobbed her head. "A few

sniffles earlier, that's all. Fortunately you had a vaporizer."

"I'm lots better now." Timmy eyed the doctor warily. "Mommy, did you know colds get hungry?" He patted her knees to gain her attention. "That's how come you have to feed them."

"No, I didn't know that," Dani murmured.

"I'd better check on that caramel." Carrie beamed at Douglas Naditch, who had been single all his fifty-two years, and somehow managed to feel her way to the kitchen without ever taking her eyes off the physician.

Dani pressed her fingers against her forehead. "Excuse me, doctor. I don't mean to be rude, but what are you doing here?"

"I'm making a house call." Stating the obvious, he reached for a piece of the fragrant cinnamon toast Carrie made. Unable to resist, Gene sat opposite Doctor Naditch and helped himself to a slice.

"A house call for whom?" Exasperated, Dani had to restrain herself from snatching the toast out from under the noses of the two men.

"I don't charge any more for late calls." Douglas winked at Gene. "Besides, the examination took awhile. Got to be thorough in cases of suspected frostbite."

"Frostbite? What—"

"Mommy—" Timmy tugged on Dani's coat. "Carrie said I have to wait for tomorrow to have my caramel apple. Can I have it tonight instead?"

"How many of those apples is she making?" Gene asked.

"Don't know," Doug answered around a mouthful of toast.

"Can I, Mommy? Can I?"

"Just a minute, pup. Who has frostbite?!" Dani raised her voice to indicate she wanted to be answered *now,* and both Gene and Doug turned toward her.

"*Suspected* frostbite," the doctor reiterated. "And he didn't."

"He." Dani's mouth grew suddenly dry. "He wh-wh-wh—"

"Who?" her father finished for her.

"Your handyman. Resting comfortably now, but his leg's going to hurt like a son of—" He glanced at Timmy. "Sorry. He'll be in some pain tomorrow. I left a few tablets, but you'll want to get to the drugstore tomorrow and—"

Dani was striding through the living room, her pace quickening with each step, before Dr. Naditch could finish his sentence. She headed for the attic stairs, but Timmy, who was dogging her steps, said, "Sam's in my room, Mommy. I gave him my bed, and I'm sleeping in Granpop's room tonight."

Dani stopped short when she reached the door to Timmy's bedroom. *He was there.* She'd been half-afraid it wasn't true, but Sam was there, indeed, sleeping in her son's twin bed. A shadow of stubble darkened his cheeks and chin. As he slept, his chest lifted with intermittent snores.

Dani stood in the doorway, aching to go in and wake Sam up, but she was reluctant to disturb him. Timmy had no such qualms. He charged into the room, tumbled onto the bed and jiggled Sam's arm. "Sam! Sam, get up."

Dani took a hasty step into the room and whispered, "Honey, no! Don't wake him."

"But, Mommy, he said to wake him up when the apples were ready."

Dani gestured for her son to leave the room with her, then nearly jumped when a husky voice rumbled groggily, "He's right, I did."

Sam was awake. And staring right at her.

Dani's breath quickened. Fatigue made Sam's eyes puffy. He seemed to have developed a few new lines overnight, too, but to Dani, he'd never looked more handsome.

"Sam, the apples are done...almost." Timmy bounced happily on the bed. Sam winced and placed a gentle hand on the boy's knee.

"Why don't you check on them, honey," Dani suggested, addressing her son, but finding it impossible to break eye contact with Sam. "If they're ready, tell Carrie I said you can have one."

"Oh, boy! I'll bring you the biggest one, Sam, 'cause you're sick."

"Thanks, troop."

Timmy hopped off the bed and raced down the hallway.

Dani and Sam stared at each other. There was so much to say, so much she wanted to ask, but the only words that came to mind were, "You're back."

Sam nodded somberly, sitting up with obvious discomfort. "Do you mind?"

Dani stared at him. The question proved irrefutably that men really were from Mars, and women from Venus. "Why is Dr. Naditch here?" She took a couple more steps into the room, checking the impulse to sit on the bed the way she would have done if Timmy were the patient. Recalling her son's words, Dani asked with concern, "Are you sick?"

Sam's mouth lifted in an ironic quirk. "No, not *sick*," he said. "Just stupid." He ran his fingers through his chestnut hair, then looked at Dani with rueful sincerity. "I can be that sometimes. Pretty damn stupid."

"I guess we all can," she said softly. "Sam, what's going on? I thought you left. Why is the doctor here? When did you get back? What's—"

She stopped when Sam patted the mattress. "Sit down will you? I'd come to you, but my leg..."

"Your leg?" Dani crossed to him immediately. When she hesitated, not wanting to sit if it might jostle and cause him pain, Sam reached for her hand and pulled her down.

"It'll be fine," he said, nodding toward his hip. "Just stiffened up from the cold, and I walked too far on it. That's all."

Dani's eyes widened. "Where were you walking in this weather?"

With his free hand, he raked his hair again. "I was driving down highway 238."

Two thirty-eight. The road out of town.

"I turned the car around and it stalled. So I walked home."

Home. Dani didn't miss his choice of words.

Sam tightened his hold on her. "Cold hands." He smiled.

That's funny, she thought. She was beginning to

feel warm for the first time all day. "You turned the car around?" she murmured. "How far did you walk?"

"A few miles."

"In the snow!"

Sam dismissed her exclamation of concern with a shake of his head. "That's not the important part."

His expression became grave and intent. "It was a long walk. I had time to figure a few things out."

Dani's heart bumped in warning. Uh-oh, was this going to be something she didn't want to hear? "Like what?"

Sam took a moment simply to look at her before he spoke. "Like how wrong I've been. I thought I was scared of you, of Timmy. Of us together." His voice cracked on the admission. "But that wasn't it at all. I was scared of me. I've been so afraid I'd fail you somehow."

As always, Sam's face bore the strength of a monument carved from granite. But beneath that, beyond it, Dani saw a vulnerability that was one hundred percent human.

"Then I was on the road," Sam continued, "and I realized that even though part of me wanted to bolt, I couldn't. I never would have. I never will, Dani." He squeezed her hands, willing her to accept both the admission and the promise. "It wasn't commitment to you that made me feel like running. What I discovered tonight is that being scared isn't the tough part. It's being ashamed that I'm scared that made me mess things up."

"Oh, Sam." The admission cost him a lot. Dani pulled a hand from his grasp and reached up to stroke the hair falling onto his brow. She didn't have to speak. The softening of the frown lines on his broad forehead told her he felt her acceptance, and the kiss he placed on the back of her hand told her how much he appreciated it.

"I have a lot to tell you, a lot to explain. Most of it can wait, but right now I want you to know that even though I had plenty of reasons for believing I wasn't a family man, not one of them had to do with you, or with Tim. One more thing I figured out tonight is that I was never ready before, partly because I was stupid and selfish and immature. And partly because I hadn't met the family I belonged to yet." Raising both her hands to his lips, he kissed each softly, one at a time. "But I have now…if you'll have me."

"Sam," Dani whispered, barely able to get any sound past the emotion in her throat. She bent forward over their clasped hands, bringing her face close to his. "Are you sure?"

"More sure than I've ever been about anything else in my life. You have no reason to believe that now, but if you let me, I'll give you a reason to believe." His gaze was unwavering; his conviction complete. "I'll give you a dozen of them."

Deep in Dani's heart, hope blossomed like the first buds of spring, sweet and pure and strong enough to have bested the winter.

"We don't have to decide anything now, you know." Habit made her counter their two steps forward with one back. She wanted to leave him a way out, should he require it. "We can take things slowly. We have time."

Sam nodded, his brow furrowing. "Hmm. A three-month trial period?"

"Right, we can be cautious."

"Discreet?" he asked. "In case things…"

"Don't work out. Right." She didn't like the sound of that, not one little bit, but she agreed. "Let's take things one day at a time, and—"

"Hey. Let's not."

"What?"

"I don't want to be *cautious*." Sam made his distaste for that notion plain. "I want to start my life with you. Marry me, Dani. Now, today. Or on Christmas Eve, or New Year's, or any time you say. I know I have a lot more explaining to do, but it's only fair to warn you that if you're willing to take a chance with me, I'm not planning on a long engagement."

The look he gave her sent shivers up her spine and fire through her veins. "Are you applying to my original ad, then? Because I have to tell you, you've got some stiff competition. There's a convict in Ohio who's coming up for parole in 2010, and I—"

The rest of her sentence was stifled as Sam pulled her close for a kiss that was hotter than any look he'd ever given her. His fingers burrowed in her hair, his palm cupped the back of her head, and words evaporated like water in the sunshine.

"On second thought," she said when they came up for air and she could think straight again, "perhaps you should make an honest woman of me. You've been trying to start something with me ever since you got here, Sam Mclean, and you haven't been here that long."

"Uh-huh," he said, eyes glinting with far too

much male pride. "I go from zero to sixty real fast once I know where I'm headed."

They grinned at each other like a couple of punch-drunk fools.

Timmy came in then, holding a humongous apple on a wooden stick. Caramel dripped down the stick and encased the fruit so heavily, it looked like someone had dipped it at least half a dozen times.

Balancing his treat, Timmy climbed onto the bed next to Dani and Sam without a moment's hesitation, as if they'd all convened here together a hundred times before.

"Lookit!" he said to Sam. "I just brought one, 'cause it's big enough for both of us." Glancing at his mother, he lowered his brow in sudden concern. "Are you going to eat any, Mommy?"

"Mmm, maybe just one tiny bite."

Timmy's brow cleared. "Okay." Generously, he held out the apple. "You can go first."

Dani did, and they took turns after that, sharing the stickiest, gooiest, most tooth-threatening treat they'd ever tasted.

They hadn't made much of a dent in it at all by the time the evening took its toll on Timmy. He curled up next to Sam, his mouth happily smeared with caramel, and was issuing little-boy snores within minutes.

Dani smoothed the russet curls off her son's forehead. Sam took her hand and drew her in gently for a much softer kiss than before, but their mouths, too, were sticky with caramel, and they pulled away licking their lips, giggling and shushing each other so they wouldn't wake Timmy.

"This really is crazy, you know," Dani said. "We're too old to fall in love this quickly. I mean...that is, assuming we are..."

"Say it."

The smile fell from her face. "In love," she whispered.

"I am." Sam's voice emerged sure and strong.

Dani nodded, tears welling in her eyes. "Me, too." Her smile returned and she drew a shaky breath. "This is almost as crazy as my ad."

"It's Christmas." Sam brushed a tear with his thumb. "Anything can happen."

"Pop says Christmas is made for new beginnings."

Sam nodded his agreement. "It'll make a great anniversary."

They fell silent then, Sam sitting up against the headboard and Dani by his side, holding hands and trading wonder-filled smiles as her son...their son slept. When Timmy stirred, they reached for him, both Dani and Sam at the same time, touching his leg and calming him instantly. They were a family already, the three of them, an unbroken circle.

Inside Dani's modest home, there was, as always, warmth and love and caring...and a little boy's toy family tucked into a storage chest, where, likely, it would stay for a while.

And outside, glowing faintly by a misty moon, there were stars...just a few, as clouds drifted by...but stars, indeed, in Idaho.

* * * * *

Available in February 1998

ANN MAJOR

CHILDREN OF DESTINY
When Passion and Fate Intertwine...

SECRET CHILD

Although everyone told Jack West that his wife, Chantal—the woman who'd betrayed him and sent him to prison for a crime he didn't commit—had died, Jack knew she'd merely transformed herself into supermodel Mischief Jones. But when he finally captured the woman he'd been hunting, she denied everything. Who was she really— an angel or a cunningly brilliant counterfeit?"

"Want it all? Read Ann Major."
—Nora Roberts, *New York Times*
bestselling author

Don't miss this compelling story available at your favorite retail outlet. Only from Silhouette books.

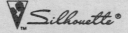

Look us up on-line at: http://www.romance.net

PSAMSC

Take 4 bestselling love stories FREE

Plus get a FREE surprise gift!

Special Limited-time Offer

Mail to Silhouette Reader Service™

3010 Walden Avenue
P.O. Box 1867
Buffalo, N.Y. 14240-1867

YES! Please send me 4 free Silhouette Romance™ novels and my free surprise gift. Then send me 6 brand-new novels every month, which I will receive months before they appear in bookstores. Bill me at the low price of $2.67 each plus 25¢ delivery and applicable sales tax, if any.* That's the complete price and a savings of over 10% off the cover prices—quite a bargain! I understand that accepting the books and gift places me under no obligation ever to buy any books. I can always return a shipment and cancel at any time. Even if I never buy another book from Silhouette, the 4 free books and the surprise gift are mine to keep forever.

215 BPA A3UT

Name	(PLEASE PRINT)	
Address	Apt. No.	
City	State	Zip

This offer is limited to one order per household and not valid to present Silhouette Romance™ subscribers. *Terms and prices are subject to change without notice. Sales tax applicable in N.Y.

USROM-696

©1990 Harlequin Enterprises Limited

Bundles of Joy

Babies have a way of bringing out the love in everyone's hearts! And Silhouette Romance is delighted to present you with three wonderful new love stories.

October:
DADDY WOKE UP MARRIED by Julianna Morris (SR#1252)
Emily married handsome Nick Carleton temporarily to give her unborn child a name. Then a tumble off the roof left this amnesiac daddy-to-be thinking lovely Emily was his *real* wife, and was she enjoying it! But what would happen when Nick regained his memory?

December:
THE BABY CAME C.O.D. by Marie Ferrarella (SR#1264)
(Two Halves of a Whole)
Tycoon Evan Quartermain found a *baby* in his office—with a note saying the adorable little girl was his! Luckily next-door neighbor and pretty single mom Claire was glad to help out, and soon Evan was forgoing corporate takeovers in favor of baby rattles and long, sultry nights with the beautiful Claire!

February:
Silhouette Romance is pleased to present ON BABY PATROL by
Sharon DeVita, (SR#1276), which is also the first of her new
Lullabies and Love series. A legendary cradle brings the three rugged Sullivan brothers unexpected love, fatherhood and family.

Don't miss these adorable Bundles of Joy, only from
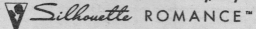
Silhouette ROMANCE™

Look us up on-line at: http://www.romance.net   BOJS-J

CHRISTINE FLYNN

Continues the twelve-book series—36 HOURS—in December 1997 with Book Six

FATHER AND CHILD REUNION

Eve Stuart was back, and Rio Redtree couldn't ignore the fact that her daughter bore his Native American features. So, Eve had broken his heart *and* kept him from his child! But this was no time for grudges, because his little girl and her mother, the woman he had never stopped—could never stop—loving, were in danger, and Rio would stop at nothing to protect *his* family.

For Rio and Eve and *all* the residents of Grand Springs, Colorado, the storm-induced blackout was just the beginning of 36 Hours that changed *everything!* You won't want to miss a single book.

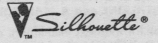

Available at your favorite retail outlet.

Look us up on-line at: http://www.romance.net

36HRS6

Welcome to the Towers!

In January
New York Times bestselling author

NORA ROBERTS

takes us to the fabulous Maine coast mansion
haunted by a generations-old secret and introduces
us to the fascinating family that lives there.

Mechanic Catherine "C.C." Calhoun and hotel magnate
Trenton St. James mix like axle grease and mineral
water—until they kiss. Efficient Amanda Calhoun finds
easygoing Sloan O'Riley insufferable—and irresistible.
And they all must race to solve the mystery
surrounding a priceless hidden emerald necklace.

Catherine and Amanda

THE Calhoun Women

**A special 2-in-1 edition containing
COURTING CATHERINE and A MAN FOR AMANDA.**

Look for the next installment of
THE CALHOUN WOMEN with Lilah and Suzanna's
stories, coming in March 1998.

Available at your favorite retail outlet.

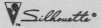

Look us up on-line at: http://www.romance.net   CWVOL1

As seen on TV!
Free Gift Offer

With a Free Gift proof-of-purchase from any Silhouette® book,
you can receive a beautiful cubic zirconia pendant.

This gorgeous marquise-shaped stone is a genuine cubic
zirconia—accented by an 18" gold tone necklace.

(Approximate retail value $19.95)

Send for yours today...

compliments of ▼ *Silhouette*®
™

To receive your free gift, a cubic zirconia pendant, send us one original proof-of-purchase, photocopies not accepted, from the back of any Silhouette Romance™, Silhouette Desire®, Silhouette Special Edition®, Silhouette Intimate Moments® or Silhouette Yours Truly™ title available at your favorite retail outlet, together with the Free Gift Certificate, plus a check or money order for $1.65 U.S./$2.15 CAN. (do not send cash) to cover postage and handling, payable to Silhouette Free Gift Offer. We will send you the specified gift. Allow 6 to 8 weeks for delivery. Offer good until December 31, 1997, or while quantities last. Offer valid in the U.S. and Canada only.

Free Gift Certificate

Name: _____

Address: _____

City: _____ State/Province: _____ Zip/Postal Code: _____

Mail this certificate, one proof-of-purchase and a check or money order for postage and handling to: SILHOUETTE FREE GIFT OFFER 1997. In the U.S.: 3010 Walden Avenue, P.O. Box 9077, Buffalo NY 14269-9077. In Canada: P.O. Box 613, Fort Erie, Ontario L2Z 5X3.

FREE GIFT OFFER   084-KFD
ONE PROOF-OF-PURCHASE
To collect your fabulous FREE GIFT, a cubic zirconia pendant, you must include this
original proof-of-purchase for each gift with the properly completed Free Gift Certificate.

084-KFDR

SILHOUETTE WOMEN KNOW ROMANCE WHEN THEY SEE IT.

And they'll see it on **ROMANCE CLASSICS**, the new 24-hour TV channel devoted to romantic movies and original programs like the special **Romantically Speaking—Harlequin™ Goes Prime Time.**

Romantically Speaking—Harlequin™ Goes Prime Time introduces you to many of your favorite romance authors in a program developed exclusively for Harlequin® and Silhouette® readers.

Watch for **Romantically Speaking—Harlequin™ Goes Prime Time** beginning in the summer of 1997.

If you're not receiving ROMANCE CLASSICS, call your local cable operator or satellite provider and ask for it today!

ROMANCE CLASSICS

Escape to the network of your dreams.

See Ingrid Bergman and Gregory Peck in *Spellbound* **on Romance Classics.**

©1997 American Movie Classics Co. "Romance Classics" is a service mark of American Movie Classics Co.
Harlequin is a trademark of Harlequin Enterprises Ltd.
Silhouette is a registered trademark of Harlequin Books, S.A.   RMCLS-S-R2